Panhandler Tales: Short Stories

By Wake Cruise

D1315288

This book is a work of fiction. Names, characters, places, businesses, and incidents are either the product of the author's imagination or are used fictitiously. Any resemblance to actual persons, living or dead, and events is coincidental.

Table of Contents

Diego: The Handsome Panhandler

By Wake Cruise

Chapter 1: Jerry

Jerry travels into Chicago from Oak Park every weekday for work. The drive takes him about half-an-hour on a good day and up to 50 minutes on a bad day when he is stuck in traffic. Beyond his abrasive morning alarm clock, he becomes more awake when he often sees the very attractive man who is assigned to the parking space next to his in the apartment's garage. Though groggily, Jerry always says, "Good morning," to the man who he still doesn't know by name. The man, who says no more than "morning" in return, brings his young son to the car and straps him in the back seat. The handsome dad stands about five-feet and seven-inches tall, has a trim and very athletic build, and has a clean-cut appearance. Jerry figures that one of this man's household duties is to drop the child off at daycare on his way to work. This man, who is the first to delight Jerry's awakening eyes most days, always enters the garage with his crisp white dress shirt only partially buttoned as it hangs out of his trousers. Jerry is not one to cruise a father when he is with his child, but it isn't beyond him to fantasize about seeing the man dress, or better yet, undress.

Jerry sets his radio to Chicago's WBBM-AM radio to listen to the latest local news, which often details where Chicago's overnight shootings occurred, as well as the day's weather forecast and the traffic report, while allowing the young dad parked next to him plenty of time to leave first. After Jerry pulls out of the garage in his blue 2020 Forte Kia, he drives to nearby Harlem Avenue and turns south to where he stops at Dunkin', which is just south of the Harlem-Lake transit train track underpass. Once there, Aadrik, who is a gorgeous dark-skinned Indian with engaging dark eyes and a full head of meticulously combed black hair, pours Jerry's large cup of black coffee and bags two Boston cream doughnuts. Jerry's order is as constant as the dollar he leaves in Aadrik's tip jar. Though Jerry is weight and health conscious, he allows himself this strong dose of caffeine and sugar once a day. He figures he has the rest of the day to burn the calories off, especially with his daily jog or time on his treadmill every evening.

While sipping his hot coffee and slowly eating one of his doughnuts, he heads further south on Harlem to the Dwight D. Eisenhower Expressway, numerically the I-290 expressway. By 7:10 every morning, he is headed east on the expressway until he exits at Damen Avenue to drive north. It is his chosen route to get to his office in Chicago's West Loop. He has worked as an accountant at a tech-consulting firm ever since he earned his Bachelor's Degree from the University of Chicago three years ago. If he were to travel further east on the expressway toward Chicago's Loop before exiting the expressway to head north, he would very possibly end up sitting in traffic rather than arriving to work on time. That's why he gets off at Damen.

Chapter 2: Diego

For the past half-year, Jerry has also enjoyed his current route to work because of the man he sees on Damen Avenue most every morning. Like clockwork, when Jerry exits at Damen and turns left to travel north, he sees two men at the first traffic light. They are either in the middle of the street or just off to the right. One is selling newspapers and the other one is panhandling. Since April, for the past five months, Jerry has been particularly interested in the man who panhandles. Even if it involves disrupting traffic, Jerry briefly stops his car, exchanges several words and smiles with the man, and gives him change and a Boston cream doughnut. To Jerry, the panhandler, who calls himself Diego, is the most handsome man he has ever seen. That is why Jerry goes beyond the handouts he gives to any other panhandler and treats Diego to breakfast, too. If this man of his ongoing desires happens to not be there, Jerry treats himself to the second doughnut. However, practically every morning, Jerry has only one doughnut because Diego is usually there to receive the other one.

Although Jerry and Diego have only had brief encounters each day they see one another, they have learned quite a bit about one another through time. Diego knows that Jerry lives in the near western Chicago suburb of Oak Park, is an accountant who does the books at a tech consulting company in Chicago's West Loop, has attended the University of Illinois, is 25 years old and single, and has about five more years to pay on his car. Jerry knows that the man's name, Diego, is actually a knick-name that his Chicago acquaintances have given him. There are two reasons for the knick-name. First, Diego is from San Diego, California. He arrived in Chicago a year ago last July. The second reason is that he has a prominent tattoo down his upper right arm that colorfully and quite artistically says, "San Diego." Through verbal exchanges, Jerry knows that Diego has other tattoos. He has let Diego know that he would be interested in seeing all of them sometime, as Jerry has somewhat of a tattoo fetish. This come-on apparently doesn't bother Diego in the slightest. Though he is modest about his good looks, he is accustom to women and men coming on to him. With his five-feet and nine-inch stature, muscular build, wide smile accompanied by thick lips across his light caramel-colored face, a prominent dimple in the center of his left cheek, and his always clean-cut black hair, he understands the positive reactions he receives from people. Jerry also learns that Diego is single, lives alone, and is just a half-year younger than he is. Born in the same year, Jerry was born in

January and Diego was born in July. When they discovered their identical ages, Jerry jested, "You missed one hell of a great six months, boy."

Of course, there are some things that Diego hasn't told Jerry and his other Chicago acquaintances. Due to a criminal record of past drug-abuse in San Diego that has followed him to Chicago, he has found it impossible to find a decent steady job. Yet, with his personality and ability to do manual labor, he has had temporary jobs in house construction on very rare occasions. When he lands a job, his bosses pick him up at his panhandling intersection since he has been camping out a short distance to the southwest during his extended transiency. A couple of months ago, he moved from Douglass Park near Sacramento Avenue and Roosevelt Road to his current location near 13th Street and Oakley Avenue. He has claimed a swath of dark green grass between two rows of trees, which have gone undisturbed by other homeless persons.

When he first got to Chicago, he tried a couple missions. However, like many people who end up on the streets instead of remaining in a shelter, Diego didn't like the rules, which he found to be restrictive, and the crowded conditions. While getting out of the mission at an early hour didn't bother him much, he didn't care for the nightly curfew. Additionally, he didn't like some of the men at the shelter due to their thievery and lack of personal hygiene. At the end of last winter when the temperatures began to rise, he went off alone with no more than a backpack, a change of clothing, a few personal items, a sleeping bag, and two blankets. He started his outdoor living on the south side of Ogden Avenue in Douglas Park, and then moved to the far north side of Douglass Park, which is on the north side of Ogden. He quickly learned where to get food and clothing donations. He also found the churches that allow him to wash the street life off himself every day or so. To the naked eye, one does not know Diego lives outdoors. Furthermore, he doesn't talk about it to anyone who hasn't witnessed him living in such a manner.

Fearful that Diego may disappear, as panhandlers most often do, Jerry has given Diego his phone number on several occasions. Each time, the insinuation is that Jerry wants him to call so they can go out. "Call me and leave a message. I can pick you up somewhere and take you to dinner," Jerry has told him. "Thanks," says Diego, but he has yet to call. With the cooler weather about to set in as fall quickly approaches, Jerry is concerned that he won't see Diego as often. By the time winter hits, he thinks, Diego may disappear entirely. Therefore, on this particular morning, when he hands Diego his phone number again, he has a message on the slip of paper with his name and number. It says, "Call me, Diego. I'm interested! Let's do dinner."

Chapter 3: The Phone Call

Late that afternoon, Jerry gets a phone call from a number that he does not recognize. Fearing telemarketers, he doesn't answer the call. Then a voice message comes through. Still thinking it is a telemarketer, he doesn't listen to the message immediately. However, when a text message follows the voice mail message, he investigates. He knows that telemarketers usually don't leave a voice message and a text. When Jerry takes a minute to read the text and listen to the message, the messages say, "It's Diego. Don't call back since it's not my phone. Please answer when I call back in five minutes or so." When another call comes in, Jerry answers, "Diego?" "Hey, Jerry. Sorry I took so long to finally call. I can see you tonight if you want." Ecstatically, Jerry returns, "Thanks for calling. Sure. I get off work at five o'clock and can meet you anywhere. Where will you be?" "I'm near a park in Pilsen right now. How about we meet at the corner of 18th Street and Damen?" asks Diego. "Perfect," says Jerry, and then adds, "I can be there by five-twenty, depending on traffic. We can do dinner." After a pause, he uncertainly says, "And hopefully we can go for a ride." Diego says, "Thanks, Jerry. Oh, and don't call this number. I'm obviously using somebody else's phone since I don't have one." "Okay. See you in a little while," says Jerry.

At the office, Jerry heads to the washroom with his toothbrush and other personal items that he keeps in his bottom desk drawer. He wants to make a good impression on him. Once leaving at five o'clock and heading to Damen and 18th Street, he begins thinking of where he can take Diego to impress him the most. Of course, it will have to be a place where no jackets are required because neither of them will be wearing a suitcoat. Then, on second thought, he thinks that he should take Diego to a very casual place. After all, he doesn't want to mislead Diego into thinking that he is wealthy. Jerry makes more than enough money at his job to get by with his current living situation and expenses. However, by no means is he wealthy.

Arriving at the intersection of 18th and Damen, Diego is standing on the southwest corner by the park. Jerry turns left and curbs his car as he taps the horn. Diego approaches and gets in the car. "Nice inside your car, Jerry." "Thanks. And to think it will be all mine after five more years of payments," laughs Jerry. "Well, at least you have good credit to buy it," says Diego. "That's true," says Jerry, and then he asks, "Any kind of restaurant in particular that you'd like to go to?" "Other than fast food places, taco trucks, and a couple carry-out diners, I don't know any restaurants," laments Diego. "Well, then, I'll have to think of something. You like burgers, Mexican food, pizza? What's your pleasure?" offers Jerry. "All of the above," laughs Diego, and then seriously adds, "I really like the Mexican food I've had in this area." "Great. I haven't been to one of my favorites in a while. It's near Halsted and Roosevelt. A place called Lalo's. Heard of it?" asks Jerry. "No, I haven't," says

Diego. "Well, let's go there. It's great. I love their tacos and chips," says Jerry.

Once at Halsted Street, Jerry parks and feeds the meter with his credit card to avoid a parking ticket. He pays for 90 minutes, thinking that should be more than enough time for their dinner. He leads his dinner guest along Halsted Street and heads east on West Maxwell Street to arrive at Lalo's. Fortunately, they are immediately seated at a booth, a good distance away from the long and crowded bar. A live singer is singing in Spanish while playing a guitar. Unfortunately, the singer's microphone is turned up much too loud. This disappoints Jerry somewhat because he really wants to be able to talk comfortably with Diego to get to know him much better. Diego is impressed by it all, though. He was telling the truth when he told Jerry that he only goes to fast food places, taco trucks, and carryout diners. He hasn't sat down inside a restaurant to eat since he was in San Diego. What he doesn't tell Jerry is, more times than not, he goes to churches and soup kitchens known for feeding less fortunate people. He also walks to a food truck that supplies free food in Pilsen every Thursday evening. Even when he can afford eating elsewhere, Diego is frugal with the small amount of cash he has on hand. He is terrified of being totally broke, as he sees so many other homeless people on the streets of Chicago.

"Order whatever you want, Diego. It's on me," says Jerry. Politely shy, Diego waits for Jerry to order first and then tells the waitress, "I'll have the same." Therefore, each of them has a three-taco dinner, which comes with a complementary cup of beef vegetable soup on this particular night, as well as Mexican rice and refried beans. Jerry only drinks water with his dinner but encourages Diego to get whatever he wants to drink. Though Diego enjoys coffee, he insists water is fine for him, too.

The two are very comfortable and open with one another. Diego gives his impression of his first fourteen months in Chicago. Though his life has been rough here, he is positive and doesn't complain. Of course, he admits that he wishes he could find a full-time job so he can afford to rent a room or, better yet, an apartment. "You don't have a place in the city?" asks Jerry. "No, I guess I never mentioned that because I thought it was obvious," said Diego. Then he adds, "I stayed at the Pacific Garden Mission on Canal Street when I first got to Chicago, but I left some time ago." "Why?" asks Jerry. Diego admits, "I tell people that it was too crowded and I didn't care for the other people there. Truth is, though, that I just prefer to be alone. I've become a loner since I got to Chicago." He doesn't admit to Jerry that he felt that he was expected to join the drug addiction program at the facility, and he doesn't want to do so just yet.

Jerry talks about his small, one-bedroom apartment as if to give an excuse as to why he lives alone. Even though Diego has noticed the suggestions that Jerry might be gay, he asks, "So, you have a girlfriend?"

"No," says Jerry without apology or explanation, and then asks, "Do you, Diego?" "Nope. Had one in San Diego, but it didn't turn out so well after I got in trouble," he admits. "Sorry to hear that," says Jerry, and then sincerely asks, "May I ask what kind of trouble you got into?" Diego looks Jerry in the eye to see his reaction as he honestly responds, "A drug addiction." Hearing that a person on the street has a drug addiction is nothing shocking or new to Jerry. Therefore, he doesn't react other than to ask, "That still a concern for you?" "Not really. Pretty much learned my lesson. But drugs are hard to avoid in Chicago. They are everywhere, you know?" says Diego. "Yes, they are. Many people I encounter when cruising the streets are addicted. And you're right. The availability can make it tough to say no," Jerry concludes on the subject, as Diego returns, "Sure does." Then Diego asks, "You cruise around a lot?" "My favorite pastime. I love driving around with so much to see on the city streets," says Jerry. He doesn't mention that he most often cruises around with his eyes searching for sex with handsome men.

Jerry thinks to suggest different programs that he knows are available to drug addicts in the city. Yet, he doesn't talk about them, not yet anyway. He has never had success with getting any of his street acquaintances to enter a drug rehabilitation program or to seek any other type of help with their drug habits. He figures that when and if they are serious about quitting drugs, they will easily find assistance themselves. They aren't ready to shake their habits yet, he figures. His encounters with men such as Diego are for possible friendships as well as for good dates when they are attractive.

Jerry and Diego both know that Jerry could take Diego home for the night and let him sleep on the floor, on the couch, or with Jerry in his bed. However, the conversation doesn't go in that direction and neither of them has the nerve to make such a suggestion. They've seen one another about five times a week for the past several months, but they haven't had a conversation that has lasted more than a half-minute until now. They scarcely know one another. Yet both of them are enjoying this dinner as a good start for becoming more acquainted.

Jerry wants to cut to the chase and say, "You're so damn handsome, Diego. You know what I want, don't you?" Diego wants to say, "I think I know what you meant when you wrote that you're interested in me on that note this morning. Tell me exactly what you mean so I can be sure." However, neither one of them says what's on their minds. Not yet, anyway.

Chapter 4: The Ride

On this nice night with a clear sky and the temperature hovering around 75 degrees, Jerry offers to take Diego for a ride into Chicago's Loop, which is the downtown area of the city. Though Diego has been in Chicago for over a year, he hasn't spent any time away from Little Village and its neighboring neighborhoods of Lawndale to its north and Pilsen to its east. Therefore, he anxiously accepts the offer to see parts of the city that he has only seen and read about in books and on the Internet. From his outdoor living locations, he has seen Willis Tower stand tall in the distance. "I'd really like to see Willis Tower up close," he tells Jerry, and then adds, "I've read so much about it, including how people still want to call it Sears Tower." "I've been in it a few times," says Jerry, "but I've never gone to the top to see the view from up there." Then he pronounces, "Maybe another day we can go downtown earlier, go inside Willis Tower, and go up to the Skydeck, though I think it costs about twenty-five dollars per person to go up there." As they head into Chicago's Loop, Diego cranes his neck to look skyward at the tall buildings. "I'm surprised there isn't more traffic," he says. "People clear out of the Loop fairly quickly after work," explains Jerry, and then adds, "Since it's almost seven-thirty and getting dark out, most people who work downtown are probably back home by now. The later it gets, the easier it is to drive around in the Loop. We timed this ride pretty good." "Is the lake far from here?" asks Diego. "Straight ahead," says Jerry, then offers, "Let's take you for a ride up Lake Shore Drive. There will be more traffic there, though." Jerry is right. When they get to Lake Shore Drive and head north, they join a constant flow of traffic. Diego looks out his passenger's side window to see Lake Michigan just before the view turns dark at nightfall.

Jerry exits off Lake Shore Drive at Belmont Avenue and drives west to Halsted. He says, "If you're not in a hurry to get back, I can take you through North Halsted. It used to be called Boystown." When Diego doesn't react, Jerry asks, "Have you heard of the area?" "Nope, I have no idea where we are," says Diego. "North Halsted is where a lot of gays and lesbians live. The area is full of gay bars and businesses," says Jerry. "You come here much?" asks Diego. "I've been here a few times, but I don't come often," says Jerry. Then he explains, "We are far north in the city, which is out of my way. Since I live west of the city and work in the West Loop, I don't get far north or far south very often." "Okay. There's a big gay area in San Diego," he offers. Surprising to Jerry, he adds, "The Hillcrest area of San Diego is very gay. I lived fairly close to it." "So you went to gay bars and businesses?" asks Jerry. "No, but I've been past them," says Diego. "For one thing," he then adds, "the area is kind of expensive for me. My family gets by, but we were never rich." Jerry wants to continue this conversation to pry into Diego's attitudes toward gays as well as his experiences, if any. However, he doesn't know what to say.

Next, when Jerry gets to Clark Street on Halsted, he veers left to drive past Wrigley Field where the Chicago Cubs play baseball. Diego really enjoys circling around the ballpark, as he is an avid baseball fan. Even though Jerry is from this area, Diego reveals through his comments that he knows a lot about baseball and the Cubs. "Have you been by Sox Park on the South Side? You stay fairly close to it," says Jerry. "No," returns Diego, "I don't know where it is." "I'll take you by it another time when we take a drive through the South Side," says Jerry, in an effort to let Diego know that he wants to spend more time with him in the future. After cutting back east along Addison, Jerry turns south on Halsted. With nighttime haven fallen, people are out on the streets, going bar to bar. Jerry figures Diego will notice the heavy concentration of men, and he might even see some men walking hand in hand. Sure enough, Diego says, "This area reminds me of San Diego a little bit." "Like I said," says Jerry, "this is North Halsted, the gay area." "So lots of gay dudes like the Cubs?" asks Diego. "I have no idea," says Jerry.

"Want to stop and have a drink at one of these bars?" asks Jerry. "Not really. I don't do bars or clubs. Never have," says Diego. Then he asks, "Do you?" Jerry admits, "I've been to a few bars throughout Chicago and Oak Park, but I'm not a drinker or a bar person either." To spend as much time as possible with Diego on this night, Jerry takes the length of Halsted all the way back down to Roosevelt Road, talking about DePaul University, Chicago's Greektown, and finally his time as a student at the University of Illinois as he passes his alma mater in University Village. "I wasn't a great student," confesses Jerry, "but I got my degree." "I took a few classes after high school, but I never finished college," says Diego. Then he says, "It just wasn't for me. It was another way I disappointed my Dad, I guess. I only gave it a shot 'cause he always assumed I'd go to college. He had to have known that I hated school, but that didn't stop him from expecting me to continue my education after high school." He concludes with a laugh, "He unrealistically thought that I would get a baseball scholarship at some school, but I was only a great baseball player in his mind, not in reality. I was good for a high school player, but that was all."

"I can relate to the high expectations," says Jerry. "My Mom thought I was a great student, but I didn't care for studying. I mean, I always did what I needed to do to get a passing grade in my classes, but that was all." Unexpectedly, Diego asks, "You said you don't have a girlfriend, right?" Jerry tenses up as if he isn't ready for this subject to be discussed, but he admits, "That's right" The topic remains there without any further comment about it from either of them.

"Why don't you show me where you go at night," says Jerry. Fearful of Jerry's reaction, Diego hesitantly says, "I live outdoors." Jerry successfully tries not to react to the revelation. Diego continues, "Been a long day. I'm tired and can go back there now unless you have more places to go," Diego says. "No, I need to get home and get some sleep for tomorrow, too," returns Jerry, and then adds, "I want to see where you stay so I'll know where to find you when I'm driving around late at night." Diego currently stays in an open, grassy area just east of Western Avenue, a couple of blocks off the busy intersection of Ogden Avenue and Roosevelt Road. Jerry follows Diego's navigation instructions and curbs his car along 13th Street when Diego tells him to do so. Diego points to a small patch of trees and says, "I've been staying here for some time now." "Alone?" asks Jerry. "Yes, I stay alone," says Diego. Jerry taps his horn three times and says, "That's the sound you'll hear when I stop by." Diego opens the door, turns to Jerry, and embarrassingly begs, "I hate to ask since you've been so generous with dinner and the ride around the city." Before Diego even finishes his request, Jerry says, "Of course." He takes a five-dollar bill out of his wallet. As he hands it to Diego, he says, "I can give you this." "Thanks, you're too good, Jerry," Diego admits. "I told you," Jerry concludes as he lightly squeezes Diego's left forearm, "I'm interested." "Thanks," repeats Diego, while still not exactly sure of what Jerry means when he says he is interested in him.

Chapter 5: Friends

The next morning, Jerry's routine remains the same. However, he has more energy and a smiling heart as he begins his day due to the decent time he had with Diego the previous night. He sees the sexy papa in the garage and greets him with more gusto. When Jerry sees Aadrik at Dunkin', he greets him in a more spirited tone of voice and tips him two dollars instead of one. When he sees Diego at the stop light on Damen, his smile is bigger than usual as he hands him his doughnut and says, "Enjoyed going out with you last night and getting to know you better, Diego." "Same here. Let me know when we can take another ride," Diego says, to which Jerry replies, "Call me or tell me when I see you here." "You could just stop by my house," jests Diego. Then he seriously adds, "I'm usually back there after eight o'clock."

At work, Jerry's thoughts are on Diego all day. He relives their conversations, and his mind's imprints of Diego's handsome face and smile won't go away. He is embarrassed and somewhat annoyed by his schoolgirl crush on the man. In a way, he hopes the feelings pass. In another way, he hopes the feelings remain. He is in a very good mood with this developing friendship with Diego. It's a mood he rarely experiences.

Midafternoon, Jerry gets a call on his phone. Not recognizing the phone number, he ignores the caller by not answering. A voicemail comes in. When he listens to it, he hears Diego telling him, "It's Diego. Nothing serious, but I'm at the Emergency Room at Mount Sinai Hospital. I got hit by a car and will have a hard time getting around when they're done with me here. They're going to do x-rays to make sure nothing's broken and they've already given me painkillers. Pain was bad. I hate to bother you, but can you stop by and give me a ride when you get off work? I'll wait around the Emergency Room until six o'clock. My real name, by the way, is Jesus Alvarez. If you come and I'm still in the Emergency Room, you can ask for me by name. No rush, but I could really use a ride from here. Thanks." Immediately, Jerry finds the phone number for Mount Sinai Hospital and contacts the Emergency Room. He tells them to tell a patient named Jesus Alvarez to stay in the Emergency Room when he is released because his friend Jerry will be by to pick him up. The woman on the phone says, "Let me jot this down. Jesus Alvarez, and your name is Jerry. I will see that he gets the message."

Jerry gets to the hospital at 5:20 and sees a closed gate that says "Ambulances Only." Therefore, he drives down Ogden a block and a half and parks his car. Approaching the pedestrians' entrance to the Emergency Room, he sees Diego sitting a short distance away from the entrance with his legs stretched out in front of him. He is sitting on the concrete with his back against the wall. When he sees Jerry, he calls out to him and struggles to get to his feet. Jerry hurries over to him and picks up his walking stick that the hospital provided for him. "How you feeling?" asks Jerry. "I'm sore, but much better than I felt before." "Let me circle the car around to pick you up on the street. I'm parked about a block down." "I can make it if we take it slow," says Diego. As they walk to the car, Jerry says, "No cast. So, nothing is broken?" Diego says, "No," and adds, "Sorry about all of this." Jerry says, "You don't have to be sorry. I'm sorry it happened to you." Diego explains, "I was given a prescription for some sort of pain pills," and adds, "I have a low tolerance for pain and would like to get them before the pain-killer I'm on begins to wear off. Can we go somewhere to get it filled?" "Of course," says Jerry, and then adds, "There's a Walgreens over in Pilsen on Cermak."

"Did someone hit you on Damen?" asks Jerry. "No, I was crossing Western Avenue at Ogden to go to Burger King when a vehicle flew by and brushed my back. I hit the ground. It knocked the fucking wind outta me." Defensively he adds, "I had the right of way. I never cross that busy intersection without the walk sign on. Don't know whether the car blew the red light going south on Western or if it came from the angled turn off Ogden. As fast as it was going, he probably came straight down Western." "Did the driver stop?" asks Jerry. "No, I don't think the driver even knew I got hit," replies Diego. He then says, "A regular panhandler in the northbound lane of Western suddenly appeared and helped me get off the street. He ran into Burger King to have them call for an ambulance. When he came out, he was with a man who offered to give me a short ride to the hospital. I tried to give the man five dollars for his help but he wouldn't take it."

Though Jerry often thinks with his crotch instead of his brain when it comes to handsome men, he is too cautious to let a man he really doesn't know very well to stay at his place. Therefore, he rejects the thought of inviting Diego to stay with him. Instead, he tells himself that he will take care of Diego while leaving him at his current campout location. He makes sure that Diego is fed and has non-perishable foods to get him through the next day. "If you're able to get around at all, here's a little money to help you until I can take you for something to eat after work tomorrow," says Jerry as he finds two five-dollar bills in his wallet. "You've got that McDonald's on Ogden that is closer than the Burger King on Western. You can probably get that far?" he suggests. "I'm going to owe you bigtime," says Diego. "You owe me nothing," says Jerry, and then laughs his dirty little laugh as he softly lingers, "though I'm still interested." Diego touches his shoulder and says, "After all this, you're interested? In what?" "Not what," Jerry softly says, "but who." Their eyes lock and Diego casts a huge and satisfying grin.

Chapter 6: Revelation

For the next three days, Jerry stops by Diego's campsite after work. The first two days, Diego is there. They go to McDonald's just east of Western Avenue on Ogden, picked up a couple of Big Mac meals and sit in the grass at Douglas Park while devouring them. After picking up snacks for Diego at the Walmart Market on Cermak, he drops him off at the patch of grassy land where he stays. Jerry then heads home. On the third day, when Jerry stops by, Diego isn't there. Jerry finds a note weighted down by a big rock on top of the sleeping bag saying, "Walking slow but better. Don't know if I'll be back in time to see you. Take care." Jerry walks back to his car, gets a pen, and writes beneath the note, "Glad you're better. Call if you need anything. See you soon. P.S. – I'm interested!" After his written words, he draws a smiley face. Since it is Friday evening and they don't see one another at Diego's panhandling location over the weekend, Jerry is correct when he assumes he won't see Diego again until Monday morning.

On Monday morning, Jerry finds that he is correct. He sees Diego accompanied by his walking stick at 7:35 in the morning. Jerry turns on his car's flashing lights as vehicles honk their horns from behind. He greets Diego by shouting, "Hey, handsome, how you feeling?" "Surviving!" returns Diego. Jerry can see that he is in the same clothes he had on the last time he saw him four days ago. He also has scruffiness on his cheeks and chin, which means he hasn't shaved or had a chance to clean up since he saw him last. Wanting to help Diego get cleaned up and to help him find a change of clothes, he hurriedly asks, "Where can I pick you up after work?" "Thanks, I could use a ride to get some things," says Diego, and then adds, "I'll be at my place. Promise."

That late afternoon, Jerry arrives and finds Diego napping. Rather than wake him, Jerry leaves a note next to Diego saying, "Don't want to disturb you. I'm napping in my car on 13th Street. Come wake me." Though Jerry has a hard time sleeping in his car, he is able to relax until Diego appears at his driver's side window and says, "You could have woken me up. I've got all night to sleep. Was just tired." Something in Diego's eyes told Jerry that it was more than tiredness that knocked him out. Though he doesn't say a word about it, it looks like Diego has used some of his panhandling money to visit a drug dealer over in Lawndale.

After Diego gets in the car, he looks at Jerry's concerned facial expression and asks with paranoia, "What's wrong?" "Nothing's wrong. I just want to set things straight," says Jerry. He takes a deep breath and continues, "What you do is none of my business." After a pause, he then sternly asserts, "Except when you're with me and in my car. No drugs in my car, okay?" Diego looks like a child who has been caught with his hand in the cookie jar, and says, "I'd never put you at risk like that, Jerry. Never." "I don't think you ever would, but I just want to make sure you know the rules," says Jerry. Diego considers telling Jerry a fib, which is to say that he's out of prescription pain pills and needed something for pain. Instead, he gives Jerry a dirty smile and asks, "So even when I'm a mess, you're still interested in me?" In spite of his dirty clothes and scruffy appearance, Jerry puts his right arm around Diego's neck, draws him close and growls, "Hell yeah!" Then he seriously asks, "You hungry?" Diego echoes, "Hell yeah!" "McDonald's again? Or are you sick of their food?" asks Jerry. "Anywhere is fine," Diego says. "I never tire of their burgers," says Jerry. "Me neither," agrees Diego.

To take a short ride together, Jerry drives down Western and goes to the McDonald's on Cermak Road between Western and Rockwell. They go inside rather than use the drive-through. While Jerry orders at the counter and waits for two Big Mac meals with Coca-Colas, Diego is in the washroom. He remains in the washroom for at least ten minutes to wash up as well as he can at the sink. Using hand soap, he washes his face, hair, hands, and forearms. Then he dries himself off as well as he can at the hand dryer. With his hair still damp, he walks into the dining room and finds Jerry at a booth with their food just outside the washroom. Jerry is talking to a man at another booth across the aisle. "Vincent, this is Diego," Jerry tells the man who is surprised to see the two men together. Diego nods as Vincent gets up to use the washroom before leaving. "So you know that guy?" asks Diego. Jerry confirms, "I've seen him here when it's cold out. In addition, I've seen him at the strip mall on Western and Cermak where he opens doors for customers. He's sleeps on the bus stop benches around here." He then informs, "Once, when it was freezing out last winter, the manager was throwing him out for loitering. I bought him a cup of coffee so he could stay inside the restaurant. It worked. With a cup of coffee in front of him, the manager left him alone. That was the night I got to know him a little bit." Though Diego doesn't really know Vincent, he contributes his knowledge of him by saying, "I've seen him walking along Roosevelt Road sometimes."

This is revealing to Diego. He is thinking that maybe he isn't all that special to Jerry. Maybe he treats everyone as well as he is treating him. After all, Diego has thought that there is something about himself, maybe his good looks, his personality, or maybe his good luck that have won Jerry's attention. Vincent's appearance, as an unattractive little old man, and his lack of personality obviously aren't what would get anyone to help him. Diego doesn't tell Jerry that he occasionally has seen the awkward loner leaving a crack house north of Roosevelt near Sacramento in Lawndale. Diego and Vincent obviously do their shopping at the same place. As Diego and Jerry eat in silence, Diego's mood turns dark as he thinks he could easily end up like Vincent if he doesn't get completely off the fucking drugs.

After leaving McDonald's, Jerry takes him to a second-hand store down Cermak where Diego finds a medium-size t-shirt with the Rolling Stones logo and size 32-34 blue jeans for ten dollars. He pays for it out of his panhandling earnings for the day without asking for anything more from Jerry. From there, they walk over to the Dollar Store where he purchases Brut deodorant, a disposable Bic razor, and a bar of soap. Lastly, Diego asks Jerry to take him to a church down in Little Village, along Central Park Avenue. There, he knocks loudly on the door until a man answer. An attractive, clean-cut man, who is probably about 35 years old, answers his knocks. The Brother is dressed in black slacks, a black shirt without the white collar, and black dress shoes. He smiles broadly when he sees Diego, shakes his hand, and allows him to enter. Diego has obviously been here previously. While Diego transforms himself from a street bum to a handsome, desirable-looking human being again, Jerry takes a brisk walk up to 26th Street and circles around the area for his daily exercise. When he hears popping sounds, which are likely gunshots or firecrackers, he jogs back to his car. When he approaches, he sees Diego's trim yet muscular body leaning against the passenger's side of his car. With Diego's back to the car, Jerry sees that the medium-sized shirt fits his torso very nicely. More noticeable is the pair of blue jeans that he is now wearing with the thick leather belt he wore with the pair he had on earlier. Like the t-shirt, the jeans fit him nicely around his trim waist and in his protruding crotch. He looks like a model, thinks Jerry.

He considers saying something positive about Diego's visual transition and decides to do it.

"Wow!" he says, and sincerely adds, "Looking damn good, stud. Too good." Diego, who is surprised by the compliment, asks, "Really?" "Yes sir. You clean up real good," says Jerry, as he unabashedly looks him up and down. "Well, thank you," says Diego, and admits, "I'll take all the compliments I can get." "What did you do with your other clothes?" asks Jerry. "When I asked where I could throw them out, the Brother put them in a plastic bag and tossed it aside. He might wash them and give them away? I don't know."

Even though Jerry knows it is going to be a challenge to keep his eyes and hands off Diego if they spend much time together this evening, Jerry suggests they take a relaxing ride. "That sounds great," says Diego. As he heads to the west to the town of Cicero, he asks Diego if that church on Central Park is the place he always goes to clean up. Diego says, "Since it's far from where I'm staying, I've only been there a few times. The Brother at the church seems to like me. The first time I went there on a recommendation from another guy on the street, the Brother said I could stop by any weekday evening between 6 and 10, as that's when he answers the door to help the homeless." "So you've seen other transients there?" asks Jerry. "No," says Diego, "I haven't seen anyone else washing up when I've gone there." "Has he asked you to sleep there, too?" asks Jerry. "No," says Diego, "but he has suggested a couple of places where I could stay indoors. I told him that I prefer being on my own. When the winter weather comes, I may look into doing something else. It's a day at a time, ya know?" "Let me know before you disappear from your current place," says Jerry, and adds as he touches Diego's upper left leg, "I don't want to lose you." Without a flinch, Diego readily accepts Jerry's touch and firm squeeze. "So you're not ticklish?" he asks. "No, never been," says Diego, and adds, "With those strong hands, I bet you give a good massage." "Hmm," says Jerry, "never gave one. Let me know when you're willing to be a guinea pig." "Never had a massage," says Diego, "so I wouldn't know a good one from a bad one." "I never had one either," says Jerry, "but I imagine it's a good massage if it feels good and a bad one if it doesn't." Before dropping the subject, Jerry asserts, "I could finally see your other tattoos if I massage you." "Yes, they're on my chest and back," says Diego. At this, Jerry gets an uncomfortable, raging hard-on in his pants. When he tries to push it down with his left knuckles, Diego looks over as though he wants to be caught looking.

In Cicero, Jerry points out different businesses, especially restaurants, which he has patronized in the past. He ends up driving south of 31st Street, just west of Cicero Avenue, and reaches the train tracks where the streets don't go through to Pershing Road. Along a long fence, which separates a house's back yard from the street, he parks his car to take a piss and Diego does the same. Diego's piss is a long, strong stream, which takes him some time to complete.

"Your bladder was full," says Jerry. "Yeah," says Diego, "Drank three full glasses of water in the church. I was really thirsty." "No bread and wine?" jokes Jerry. "I would have, but the Brother didn't offer any." Diego lifts his ass off the car seat and reaches deep into his right pocket and pulls out two granola bars as he says, "He gave me a couple of these, though. Want one?" "No thanks," says Jerry, as Diego opens one to eat and puts the other back in his jeans' pocket. "Nice spending time with you, Diego, but I don't know where else to go right now," says Jerry. "We could just sit here, if you don't mind," says Diego, and as he reclines his seat a bit he says, "I'm in no hurry to get back to my place." Jerry turns the car off and reclines his seat a short distance as well. Then, however, thinking of past hassles created by the cops in Cicero, Jerry changes his mind and tells Diego, "We can sit in the car, but not here, where we might look suspicious to the cops in this town. They can be a nightmare!" Therefore, Jerry drives to the huge parking lot near Home Depot on Cicero Avenue and parks his car there.

Before long, Diego begins to snore lightly as Jerry tries to become as relaxed as his companion is. Unfortunately, he isn't used to sleeping in a public place, and he has difficulty getting relaxed enough to sleep. He figures that just laying back quietly amounts to enough rest. Before Diego wakes up some twenty minutes later, he has a natural hard-on tented in his jeans, which Jerry scarcely notices in the dim parking lot lights. It's all he can do to not start massaging Diego's crotch. Daringly, as Diego wipes his mouth with the back of his right hand and apologizes to Jerry for having fallen asleep, Jerry says, "Couldn't help but notice you got a little excited while you were napping." "Excited?" asks Diego. "Yes," says Jerry, "I looked over at you when you began gently snoring and saw a rise in your Levis." "I snored?" asked Diego, and then said, "I'm really sorry. I'm not very good company, am I?" "It's okay," says Jerry, and considers, "You're tired."

Before starting the car, Jerry thinks this may be the time to drop more clues about wanting to pleasure this gorgeous man. He says, "Speaking of erections," and pauses. "Yes?" says Diego. "Do you have much sex in Chicago?" asks Jerry. "Nada," Diego returns immediately. "Really? Don't you get blue balls? Or are you good at having wet dreams?" asks Jerry. "Wet dreams once in a while, I guess. I don't jerk off," says Diego. He feels as though he should return the questions to Jerry, but he really isn't interested in how Jerry satisfies himself. "You watch porn?" asks Jerry. "I did once in a while when I had a phone," admits Diego. Jerry grabs his phone and asks, "Which sites?" Diego reaches for his phone and says, "I can show you." He opens the browser on Jerry's phone and types "fuck videos" in the search bar. He finds a link to xvideos.com and taps on it. Holding the phone so they can both look, he taps the link to the first video. Sure enough, a man with a huge cock is fucking some woman from behind. Apparently not liking that one, Diego clicks on another video. This one, which is obviously more to his liking, shows an older, big-chested, white woman being eaten out by a young white guy. They watch as the man in the video replaces his mouth with his cock in the woman's pussy. Diego finally speaks again by saying, "For free sites, this one is the best I've found." "Doesn't get you so horny that you want to jerk off?" asks Jerry. "Nah, just like watching and wishing I were the dude getting some," says Diego.

Though not terribly interested in the video, Jerry puts his seat back up and leans over to continue watching the video with Diego. He uses the close proximity as an excuse to put his right hand on Diego's leg. "Not bad, huh?" says Diego. When Jerry doesn't respond, he asks, "What kind of videos do you like?" "I don't get into porn." "Seriously?" asks Diego. "No," asserts Jerry, and then surprises himself by cleverly saying, "I'm a doer rather than a viewer." Diego laughs, "Ha," and then asks, "What do you do?" Without hesitation, Jerry is forthright by admitting, "I like giving oral," Diego says, "Pussy-eater!" "That, too," lies Jerry. "You eat ass?" Diego asks surprisingly. "Never," says Jerry, and then asks, "Can you handle the truth?" Diego doesn't immediately respond. "Or did you already figure out the truth?" asks Jerry. Diego cautiously says, "I think I figured it out." "Did you have it figured out before now?" asks Jerry. Diego dishonestly boasts, "I figured it out the first time we talked on Damen." He sees that Jerry doesn't like this response and says, "Not really. I started wondering, though, after we talked on Damen a half a dozen times or so. "Tell me the truth," says Jerry, "Now that it's out in the open, is it a problem?" "Like I said before, lots of gayness in San Diego, and I lived there my whole life until last year. Never been a problem for me." "Ever try anything with a guy?" asks Jerry. "Nah," says Diego. Jerry puts the car in drive, looks to Diego, and says, "If you ever want to try, please let me be first in line." Though Diego doesn't exactly know what Jerry wants him to try, he nervously snickers and say, "Cool."

If Diego is going to have a sexual relationship of any type with Jerry, it needs to begin soon. Whether right or wrong, Jerry thinks it will be awkward if they become close friends first. He has only had a sexual relationship with one man, Juan, who became his close friend before the sexual relationship began. Juan, who is a Pilsen resident, and Jerry had a friendship that Jerry strongly guided into a sexual relationship. The relationship lasted 18 months. By the time Jerry had finally walked away from Juan several years ago, Juan had stripped him of his heart, his soul, his dignity, his trust in others, and more than a thousand dollars. For several years now, until getting to know Diego recently, Jerry has not been extremely generous and self-giving to any man, as he is very fearful of being used and hurt again.

Consequently, Jerry doesn't want to destroy his developing friendship with Diego by having any kind of sex or allowing himself to have strong feelings for him beyond the friendship type. Yet, at the same time, due to his tremendous physical attraction to Diego, Jerry is reluctant to destroy the momentum he has built for having some sort of sexual relationship with Diego. He is torn between either letting the close friendship with Diego grow or having good sex with him for as long as it might last. If having a sexual relationship will challenge their friendship, he thinks he shouldn't pursue that kind of relationship with Diego, as he hasn't found in the past that having sex and becoming friends mesh for him. Additionally, he has found that when he concentrates on cruising for sex, dicks are a dime a dozen in Chicago while making good friendships has been extremely difficult for him to do.

Chapter 7: Diversion

As Jerry drops Diego off at his campsite, they see that someone has dumped some things off at the side of the street. As they look through the items, a familiar saying comes to mind, which is to say that one man's garbage is another man's treasure. Diego claims two items that are useful to him. One is a large, sturdy piece of luggage. Fortunately, it is unlocked and clean inside. The other, as if a Godsend, is a tent. After kicking the other items to the curb, they carry the suitcase and tent to the clearing among the trees. Excitedly, Diego says his number one project after panhandling tomorrow morning will be to get what he needs to post the tent.

When Jerry leaves Diego, rather than heading straight home, he drives to Cermak Road to cruise. This evening's sexual talk and sexual orientation revelation with Diego, compounded by how good Diego looks after cleaning himself up at the church, has made Jerry horny as hell. He doesn't find any prospects between California Avenue and Western Avenue along Cermak. Before giving up, though, he drives to 21st Street where some locals hang out late at night in an underpass. Though it has been many months since he has picked up anyone there, he drives very slowly through the underpass in hopes of being spotted by someone who may remember him as a good, quick date. After parking a short distance west of the underpass, he gets out, stands near the curb behind his car, and takes a long piss. From the underpass, a man slowly wanders along the sidewalk. Jerry looks over his shoulder as the man approaches, then quickly zips up his pants and gets back in his car since he can't clearly see who owns the dark silhouette that is approaching him. When the man arrives at Jerry's passenger side window, his deep voice with a thick Spanish accent quietly asks, "You remember me?" Jerry turns on his dome light, looks closely at the man's face, and remembers the cute face that he hasn't seen for a year or maybe longer.

He says, "I remember your face." "Good," says the man. Jerry admits, "But that's all I remember. Where'd we meet?" The man says, "I don't remember where we met, my friend. But I remember the last time I saw you." "Where was that?" asks Jerry. In his broken English, the man says, "You find me walking late at night on Western Avenue when I gotta too much beer. You stop. You give me ride. Now you remember?" "Sorry, no, I don't," says Jerry. "No? Maybe you remember asking if you can suck my dick. When I say yes, we go behind Walmart on 23rd Street." At this, Jerry admits remembering the one time he sucked a man off while parked along the street behind Walmart. It was before cameras were installed there. The man continues, "You suck good, my friend." Jerry extends his right arm in a motion to offer his passenger's seat, and the man gets in the car. He spreads his legs and starts opening his jeans as he commands, "Drive away from the others." Jerry does as he is told to do. Then the man does he is told by reclining his car seat and angling the mirrors so he can see behind the car. Hungry as hell for the man's thick, uncut cock, Jerry bends to his right with his head facing down. Once he is in the handsome Mexican's crotch, Jerry gets a hot rush from the musky, manly scent emanating from his open jeans. He takes the man in his mouth completely and moans in delight as he savors the taste of the man's dirty cock. "Is good?" asks the handsome Mexican. "Mmm," replies Jerry as he begins bobbing his head up and down on the man's hardening penis. As the man's girth expands in Jerry's mouth, the man puts his right hand on the back of Jerry's head to anchor his sucking jaw. Then he starts aggressively moving his hips to fuck his mouth and throat. From the man's unique, pleasurable, and satisfying method of fucking throat, Jerry remembers him well. Though the man only stands about five-feet and four inches, he proportionately has the cock of a much larger man.

As Jerry works his sucking jaw on the face-fucker, he recalls some exciting details about the man inside of him. The man had previously told him that he has a wife and a baby in his apartment in the neighborhood. Having long been excited by sexy, masculine, pussy-loving, face-fucking cock, Jerry is in his cocksucker's glory as he works his skillful mouth to get the man's baby-making batter. After the man grunts, growls, and then drains his milk-filled balls inside of Jerry, he watches in delight and with appreciation as Jerry gulps all of his semen, unlike his wife has ever done. Then Jerry soothingly licks his entire shaft clean, also unlike his wife has ever done for him. When finished, Jerry sits up and says, "Mmm, you really needed that, didn't you, babe?" "Fuck, yeah. You suck too damn good, man," compliments the completely satisfied sex-lover. "You said you have a wife and a baby." "Yes," says the man, and details, "I have wife and daughter." "Wife like to suck?" asks Jerry. "Nothing," says the man, and then adds as he puts his cock back in his briefs and jeans, "You give fifty dollar last time." Without skipping a beat, Jerry lies,

"You've got me confused with another one of your cocksuckers." "Ha-ha. You funny, man. You only man who suck my dick," exclaims the man. Yet, Jerry insists, "I don't know what you're thinking of then because I'm not rich. I never have fifty dollars for dick."

After spending money on Diego in recent times, Jerry usually has less than twenty-five dollars in his wallet when he drives home at night. This night is no different, as he hands his satisfying date a ten-dollar bill. The man holds it up to the dim streetlight before them and squints to see the denomination of the bill. He pleadingly bellows, "C'mon, man, this all you got for me?" Even though the man's breath smells as though he had more than enough beer tonight, Jerry reasons, "That's more than enough for another six-pack of beer. I'll try to have more next time." At that, the man gets out of the car and starts walking back to his acquaintances in the underpass. Jerry heads home. For the first time in ages, Jerry strokes off that night while thinking of the hot, cute papa he serviced tonight instead of stroking off to his fanciful thoughts of servicing Diego.

Chapter 8: The Campsite

The next day, Jerry leaves for work earlier than he usually does. In the process, he doesn't see Diego at the first traffic light north of the I-290 Expressway on Damen. Instead, an old Black man is marching the pavement with a large, lidless, cracked McDonald's soda cup that awaits change from the passers-by. Jerry gives him two quarters and the Boston cream doughnut that he had would have given to Diego if he had been there. After work, he stops by Diego's campsite. He parks his car along 13th Street, snakes his way through the trees to find that Diego has gotten spikes to pitch and anchor the large tent to the ground. He calls out to Diego and gets no response. Diego is not there. The large suitcase is now inside the tent with an open sleeping bag and two thick blankets stretched out on top of it. Jerry goes back to his car, finds a long receipt with no writing on the back, and grabs a pen. He writes Diego a note that reads, "Stopped by. I'll be in the area for an hour or so. Try to call if you want me to come back. Later, Jerry." Jerry gets a light dinner and then goes cruising. To Jerry, having had the cute Mexican's nice dick last night is like eating sweets. When he has some, he continually wants more until he gets beyond his fill. Therefore, more than anything, he wants to suck another cock this evening.

After having a dipped beef sandwich with cheese fries and a Coca-Cola at the Portillo's Restaurant on West Taylor Street in University Village, two-and-a-half miles east of Diego's campsite, he drives through Pilsen by taking the length of Cermak Road back to his cruiser's hunting ground. Not seeing anyone interesting on the street, he circles back to 21st Street where he found the cute, cum-filled Mexican last night. Probably because of the early hour, people aren't gathered there yet. He considers heading north to North Halsted where he has occasionally gone to a couple of bars in the past. In particular, he likes stopping at Lucky Horseshoe where male dancers perform on stage. Though nursing a Coca-Cola is even pricey, likely due to the free entertainment provided by the dancers, parking is always available near the bar on weeknights since it is located at the extreme south end of the nearly mile-long strip of gay bars along North Halsted Street. Another night, he thinks, as it is a long drive north, about 10 miles and nearly a half-hour drive from where he now sits on Cermak Road. A couple of locals catch his attention outside a convenience store at Cermak and Washtenaw, but the problem is that there are a couple of men there. Ordinarily, he doesn't openly cruise more than one man at a time, and the man who he ultimately cruises must be alone. It could be different if he were on North Halsted, but he is in a neighborhood that is allegedly straight.

Just as he begins a quick jaunt to 26th Street, where he has had more than one man's success at cruising for sex in the past, his phone lights up with a call from a blocked number. He doesn't answer. Soon, a voice message comes through. The voice message says, "It's Diego. Got your note. Must have just missed you. I'm using some lady's phone at a bus stop on Roosevelt and Western. I'm going to walk back to the tent right now. Don't go out of your way, but I hope to see you if you're still around." Jerry prefers spending his time with someone he enjoys being with than cruising around alone. Therefore, he suspends his plan for cruising 26th Street and quickly heads to Diego's tent.

Before Jerry arrives, Diego takes his shirt off and stretches out on the blankets inside his tent. He remembers that Jerry said he cleans up nice the day before, and he figures he still looks fresh. Though he hasn't decided if he wants to do anything sexual with Jerry yet, he definitely wants to keep his gay friend interested in him. After all, he hasn't found any other good, generous friends as he has found in Jerry. Furthermore, he hasn't had any sex for too long, not even a decent blowjob.

When Jerry arrives, he enters the tent and leaves the flap for entering and exiting wide open. He squats down and sits next to Diego who is still laying on his blankets, naked to the waist. "Don't you look right at home?" Jerry hypothetically asks. "Want a blanket to lay on?" asks Diego, and he adds, "It's roomy in here." "I'm good," says Jerry. Then he adds, "Mmm, I get to see the hot tatts without having to give a massage." "Oh, yeah, you wanted to see them," Diego returns. Jerry reaches over to his smooth chest and runs three fingers across the wings of an eagle that is inked across his chest. "Awesome," compliments Jerry. As Diego tightens his pecs, he says, "Thanks, got it in San Diego when I was 18 years old." "Mmm," repeats Jerry, and then blatantly and suggestively adds, "More than awesome, it's hot as suck." Diego then turns on his left side to reveal his back to Jerry. On his left shoulder blade is a large, multi-colored wolf. "Suckin' hot!" says Jerry, as he touches the tatt. "And what's this over here?" he asks as he moves his hand to the other shoulder blade where a petroglyph of four interconnected spirals are tattooed. "Those are spirals that symbolize the change and journey through life," explains Diego. "Why four of them?" asks Jerry. "One for each member of my immediate family. My Mom, my Dad, my younger brother Enrique, and me. It was my first tattoo. Got it when I was 15 years old." "Damn!" gasps Jerry, and adds, "These tatts are so fuckin' hot, man!" "Glad you like them," says Diego, as he turns completely on his chest and rests his turned head toward Jerry on his forearms. Jerry continues running both of his hands over his back tattoos and asks, "Why did you choose a wolf and an eagle?" "The wolf is a survivor, and the eagle was a sign of masculine strength long ago. Now it has other meanings like wisdom, power, and spirituality," responds Diego. "Interesting. Hope you don't mind me admiring them," says Jerry. "No, go ahead," says Diego while offering, "I got the wolf three years after I got the eagle." Diego enjoys being touched by someone, as it has been a long time since anyone has come near him like this. "When did you get the San Diego tattoo on your arm?" asks Jerry. "I forgot about that one. It was the second one I got from a high school friend. I was 17 when I got it." "Were they expensive?" asks Jerry. "No, the eagle and the wolf were less than a couple hundred dollars each," says Diego, and adds, "I think I gave the guy a hundred dollars for the spirals. The tattoo artist is a friend of the family who enjoys doing his artwork. And the high school buddy who did the San Diego tatt did it for free." "Did it hurt when you got them?" asks Jerry. "Yes, especially getting the Eagle because there are a lot of nerve endings that can feel pain on the chest," says Diego, and then qualifies, "But it was worth it to me. I've always wanted tattoos, and I might get more someday."

Jerry is incredibly excited by Diego's tanned, smooth-skinned back with the tattoos of the wolf and the spirals as well as his strikingly handsome face, engaging eyes, and his head of thick, black, clean-cut hair. As the sun sets in the west, the tent quickly fades to darkness. Jerry keeps his phone engaged to produce a small amount of light while they talk. "Wanna go for a short ride?" asks Jerry. "I'm good, if it's okay with you. I'm kinda tired," says Diego. "I can go and let you get some sleep then," offers Jerry. "You don't have to go, I like the company," counters Diego. Though uncomfortable without anything but the floor of the tent under him, Jerry lays down in an effort to be more relaxed. "If I didn't have to clean up and change clothes for work in the morning, I could probably fall asleep right here," says Jerry. Diego announces, "Now is a good time to camp out. In a couple of weeks, the nights will be getting too cool for comfort." Then he suggests, "Take a day off tomorrow?" "Tempting idea, but I have a lot of work to do before the weekend, and tomorrow is already Friday," says Jerry. "It is? I lose track of the days," says Diego. Then Jerry adds, "Maybe I'll camp out tomorrow night or the next, when I don't have to be concerned about getting to work the next morning. I'll think about it." A short while later, Jerry asks, "Will you be here when I get off work tomorrow?" and offers, "Maybe we can go somewhere other than McDonald's for dinner." "Let me check my calendar," jokes Diego, and then says, "Sounds great. I'll be here." Shortly thereafter, Jerry heads home.

Chapter 9: Camping Out

Very early the next morning, Jerry packs an overnight suitcase, just in case he decides to stay overnight with Diego in the tent. He packs a dark blue t-shirt and blue jeans so that he can change out of his work clothes for the potential outing. He is also taking fresh underwear and some personal items such as a toothbrush, toothpaste, a case for his contact lenses, and contact lens solution. At the last minute, he decides to throw in a washcloth, a bar of soap, and hand towel, even though he doesn't know where he would find water to use them. Already in his trunk, he has a couple of thick blankets, which are for road emergencies as well as for sitting out at parks during Chicago summers.

Having an important project to complete that day, he drives to the city about an hour earlier than usual. Due to the early hour, he doesn't see Diego on Damen. The only person he sees in the middle of the street is the newspaper hawker. Therefore, Jerry treats himself to Diego's doughnut while deciding to have a lighter lunch today. In fact, with as much work as he needs to finish by five o'clock, he decides to skip his lunch break.

At the end of his workday, he leaves his office at the usual time, around five o'clock, with the feeling of accomplishment as he has completed his boss' demanding assignment. Anxious to enjoy dining and driving around with Diego tonight, he gets to the campsite as fast as possible. Arriving at 5:25, he sees Diego milling around near the tent. Taking advantage of the unseasonably warm temperature for early fall, Diego is attractively shirtless again. He likes seeing that Diego is clean and is wearing a fresh pair of khaki pants. Diego must have made it to the second-hand shop, Jerry figures, but he doesn't ask about it.

When Jerry approaches him, Diego extends a fist. Contrarily, Jerry reaches with an open hand. Diego obliges by opening his fist and they handshake heartily. "Finish your work?" asks Diego. "Yes. All done, so I can forget about the job for a couple days," returns Jerry. "Great," says Diego. After they enter the tent, Diego stretches one of his blankets out on the tent floor for Jerry to sit, and then he sits himself on the blanket that is draped across his unrolled sleeping bag. As Diego yawns wildly, Jerry does the same. "Looks like we're both beat," says Diego as he lays back on his blanket. Jerry lays back on his blanket and says, "I woke up long before my alarm this morning, and I never fell back to sleep. It was okay, though, because it helped me get to work early. In fact, I met my boss in the elevator on the way up to my office. If I had been any earlier, I would have had to wait for him to unlock the door." "The boss must have been impressed," says Diego. "He probably was," says Jerry, and then adds, "At the end of the day, he likes to lock up by 5:30 and get out of there. That's why I was pressed to get the project done. He began reviewing it when I left at five o'clock. Hope he has good things to say about it." "I'm sure he will," encourages Diego.

"Enough about me," says Jerry, and he inquires, "How was your day?" "The usual," says Diego, "After panhandling from about seven o'clock to nine this morning, I walked down to Cermak to shop for some clothes and to get something to eat." As he points to his clean khaki pants, he continues, "I saw these pants but didn't want to spend eight dollars on them. So, I went back to panhandle until 2:30 or so. I spend more time there on Fridays since there seems to be more traffic than other weekdays." "So you did pretty well out there?" asks Jerry. "Seventy-five dollars and 8 cents, which is good," says Diego. Stressing the middle word, Jerry compliments, "That is good!" "I turned the change into bills at the

Currency Exchange on Damen and Cermak, and decided to go back to the store to buy these pants," Diego informs. "They look good on you," compliments Jerry. Both men exhausted, the two fall silent. Diego falls asleep just before Jerry does the same.

When Diego awakens, the inside of the tent is dim but not completely dark, as the sun has not completely fallen from the western sky. Laying on his back, he runs his open palms up and down his chest and abs with his trim stomach sunken. He arcs his back slightly to run his right hand beneath his belt and down to his crotch. Having awoken with an erection, he adjusts his cock in his pants to the right for comfort's sake. After pushing the hard dick to the side, he reaches lower and scratches his balls. After a good amount of scratching and soothing rubs, he puts his fingers on the length of his cock's shaft and looks to Jerry, who is still napping. Diego thinks about the sexual offer Jerry had made previously and considers. As he gently and slowly rubs up and down his 7-inch cock, Jerry stirs. He is not fully awake, though. Diego then unbuckles his thick black leather belt, unbuttons his pants at his waist, and quietly yanks his zipper down. He takes his stiff cock out and lets it automatically stand at attention as he puts his hands behind his head. He closes his eyes for a short time before he hears Jerry stirring again. He discreetly turns his head toward Jerry and peeks through his eye slits. He scarcely can see Jerry sitting up. Diego doesn't know whether Jerry has seen his cock exposed. If he has, Jerry has chosen not to respond. Diego slowly gyrates his hips upward from his blanket. "Mmm," Jerry moans gently but not quietly. He doesn't care if Diego hears him. In fact, he hopes Diego does hear him. With Jerry's left hand resting on the tent's floor only inches away from Diego's right side, Diego reaches over and taps the hand twice. No words are needed as Jerry reaches over to Diego's cock with his right hand and gently grasps his cock. He begins gliding his hand loosely up and down the shaft as his fingers repeatedly brush past the huge crown atop Diego's cut cock. Breaking his silence, Diego softly whispers, "Do what you want."

Jerry then releases the hard shaft from his hand and kneels at the right side of Diego's crotch. He touches Diego's thick black forest of curly pubic hair with the fingers of his left hand and firmly yet gently strokes Diego's cock slowly with his fisted right hand. Shortly thereafter, Jerry moves both of his hands below Diego's crotch and separates his legs at the inner thighs. Diego accommodates Jerry by spreading his feet wide apart. Jerry then repositions himself so he is kneeling between Diego's spread legs. Diego closes his eyes in anticipation of Jerry's warm, wet mouth on his cock. Without disappointment, Jerry delivers the sensation that kindles a welcome tingling throughout Diego's body. Diego resumes the gentle gyrations of his hips as Jerry moans in ecstasy at the taste and manly scent of his man's rigid rod. Jerry, who is no stranger to deep-throating large cocks, allows Diego to enter and exit his tight throat at his desired rhythm. Soon after, Diego arcs his back as he lifts his head and reaches to the back of Jerry's head with his right hand. He guides Jerry to quicken the bobbing of his mouth on his tool. Though Jerry wants this to last and last, he accommodates Diego's need to climax by tightening his jaw and repeatedly taking Diego's cock inside of him to the base, as his upper lip and nose repeatedly hit his thick, curly patch of pubic hairs. When he hears Diego's heavy panting and slight gasps, "ooh, ooh, ooh," he bobs his sucking mouth even faster. Moments later, Diego gasps, "Stop!" as he plants both of his hands on the back of Jerry's head. Jerry blissfully feels Diego's hot spurts of tart tasting cum bolt out of his cock as they strike the back of his throat. Jerry passionately gurgles, "Mmm," and then swallows his cocksucker's reward. Then he nurses Diego's cock to recovery as he washes it clean with his hungry tongue and sucking lips. Long after Diego has lost his erection and has eased back onto his blanket with his eyes still closed, Jerry continues to use his mouth to kiss and wash the abused cock that now dangles between Diego's muscular legs. As if not to get enough of Diego, Jerry rubs his hands up and down Diego's thighs, hips, and abs. Diego finally says, "That was good." Jerry takes his mouth off Diego's cock and purrs, "It was the best ever for me. Thank you for this, Diego."

They take a ride around Chicago's River North area and share a deep-dish sausage pizza at Lou Malnati's on North Wells. After dinner, they take a long walk along Chicago's Riverwalk and then a distance up and down Michigan Avenue. After returning to Jerry's car, they drive back to Diego's tent and spend the night together. At just about the time Jerry usually sees Diego on Damen on weekday mornings, Diego awakes with his cock hard again. When Jerry awakens, he takes his position between Diego's spread legs and they satisfy one another again. When finished, Jerry says, "Thanks again, stud. I could really get used to this." Saying exactly what Jerry wants to hear, Diego returns, "I bet I could, too."

The End

The Panhandler and the Cruiser

By Wake Cruise

Chapter 1: Pablo

Pablo hit a new low in his life just before his 30th birthday. Actually, he hadn't had many lows before this time. His parents, who brought him from Mexico City to Chicago when he was three years old, took good care of him and his three siblings. After Pablo graduated from high school, he became a construction worker. Most of his work has been with projects in Chicago's Little Village and in the nearby towns of Cicero and Berwyn. When he was 24, he met Maria and they quickly fell in love. A year later, they married and became the parents of Elena a year after that. Unfortunately, the housing market in the area slumped and Pablo was nearly out of work. He took odd jobs that scarcely paid him enough to support his wife and child. With great effort, however, he managed to provide for them over the past couple of challenging years.

His world came crashing down this past August when he had planned to visit his parents one Sunday evening, as had been his custom. While bicycling the three miles to his parents' home, he got a phone call in which his mother said, "Pablo, best not stop by tonight. Nothing serious, but Papa hasn't been feeling well for a few days. I don't want you to catch it and take it home to Maria and Elena. See you next Sunday instead, honey." While bicycling back to his apartment, he stopped by La Chiquita Supermarket on 26th Street to pick up milk for Elena and a few other grocery items. Seeing Daniel, an elderly man who had worked with Pablo on the houses in the past, Pablo stopped to talk for a short while. Mostly, they discussed their difficult times without permanent employment. Approximately an hour after Pablo had left his apartment to head to his parents' house, he returned to his home to find Maria in bed with the man who lives in the upstairs apartment. Without a word, the neighbor dashed out of the apartment as Daniel began packing some of his belongings. While in shock, Pablo heard Maria tearfully and unsuccessfully apologizing. Twenty minutes later, she was alone with her daughter while Pablo was out on the street with a packed backpack and his bicycle. He has been living on the street since that night three weeks ago.

Not wanting to be anywhere near his wife, he stays several miles away from the apartment, which is located in the 2700 block of South Avers Avenue in Little Village. He claims an area where there are bushes and trees in Douglas Park near Sacramento Avenue and Ogden Avenue. Unless it is raining, that is where he is found sleeping late nights. When the early September weather doesn't agree with his homeless arrangement, he seeks shelter a mile away where there is a deep entryway to an abandoned store along Cermak Road, just east of Washtenaw Avenue. In the time that he has avoided his previous neighborhood, he has begun panhandling in front of businesses along Cermak Road. The workers at a taco diner, where he panhandles nearly every evening from nine o'clock until it closes after midnight, have taken a liking to him. They occasionally give him cleaning chores and then reward him with a light dinner and a similar meal to-go. After the employees close the restaurant to the public for the night, they allow Pablo time in the washroom to clean himself up.

On a good night, the restaurant's generous customers give him as much as $15 an hour while he panhandles. With that money, the food from the diner's employees, and a decent place to wash up every night, Pablo is relatively clean and approachable for a homeless person. From interactions with other street people throughout the day, he has learned where donated clothing can be found in Pilsen, which is the neighborhood to the east of Little Village. Always having been a very good-looking and decently groomed and dressed, Pablo is eye-catching.

When Pablo arrives to the diner or other businesses and finds other panhandlers have already claimed the location for the evening, his warm and respectable personality engages the others. Thereby, others often share the location without confrontation. Fortunate for Pablo, most evenings he has the diner location to himself. The taco restaurant has many regular customers, some of whom pick up food nearly every night. Though Pablo attempts to engage most everyone who passes by, he makes an extra effort to be personable with the diner's regular customers, as he opens the door to the diner for them. He logically assumes that a complaint from a regular customer could end the decent thing he has going for himself in front of this restaurant. Though somewhat timid and embarrassed about panhandling at first, he has quickly come to accept his current situation. Surprisingly, since he had always been a trusting person previously, he has instinctively developed a sense for who can and who can't be trusted on the streets within a short amount of time. In so doing, he keeps a safe distance from most of the transient people he encounters.

Chapter 2: John

Beyond being cautious of the street people, Pablo keeps his eyes on the people who populate his surroundings. On a slow night, while sweeping the sidewalk in front of the restaurant, he notices a man sitting in a car a short distance down the street. The man is intently watching him or maybe he is watching the diner's doorway. Discreetly keeping his eyes on the man as he sweeps and occasionally stops to open the restaurant door for customers who might give him change, he sees the man holding his phone up. Pablo can't be sure, but he is almost positive that the man is taking pictures of him. After he returns the broom and dustpan back inside the restaurant, he comes back out to the sidewalk. The man is still sitting in his car while looking toward the entrance.

Though uncomfortable in doing so, Pablo is too curious about the man who probably took his picture. He swallows his nerve and walks up to the driver's side of the white 2018 Ford Fusion with his welcoming smile. John, the man in the vehicle, casts a huge smile back at Pablo and loudly says, "Hello there." "Hello," returns Pablo, and then continues, "Are you taking pictures?" Before Pablo could add, "of me," John says, "No. Just killing time before I go to work. I park along here occasionally. Sometimes I run in the restaurant for a cup of coffee. They always make it fresh for me." Pablo thinks the man is lying about taking his picture, but he doesn't press the issue. After all, he can't prove it. After glancing at the phone, he sees a weather app open rather than a camera. Therefore, no pictures or videos are being taken now. However, Pablo still suspiciously thinks the man had taken his picture since the man had been holding the phone up too high to simply be looking at something on his phone.

John continually smiles and looks into Pablo's big brown eyes while saying, "You're new here. Haven't seen you before." "I've been coming here for a couple weeks now," replies Pablo. John asks, "You know a guy named Luis who stands out here sometimes?"

"No, I don't know any of the panhandlers by name," Pablo says. John continues, "Luis used to be here almost every night for a while, but I haven't seen him for maybe a half a year. At first, from a short distance, I thought you were him because you have the same stature." After a pause, he adds, "Though he wasn't clean-cut like you. I thought that maybe he got himself cleaned up after all this time." As a somewhat uncomfortable silence stands between them, John finally asks, "What's your name?" "Pablo," he replies. Before he asks for John's name, John quickly offers, "I'm John. Nice to meet you." "Same here," says Pablo as he extends his arm to shake hands. "Wow," says John, "nice tattoos, Pablo." "Thanks," Pablo returns, and then offers details about the tattoos John sees on his forearm. "These are family members' names," he says as he points to them, "and this one is a sketch I like." John reaches with his right arm, rubs his fingers over the inked sketch, and says, "Very, very nice." Having a man touch and compliment his tattoos is a first for Pablo. More embarrassed than uncomfortable, Pablo says, "I've got to get back to the door to make some money." He pauses to see if John will give him some change. "I don't have much change," says John. Then he quickly takes out his wallet and says, "Let me see if I have any singles." After searching his thick, black wallet with his fingers, he takes out two one-dollar bills and offers, "Here, Pablo. I've got two singles." "Thanks a lot," says Pablo, and then heads back to the front of the diner. As he heads back, John shouts, "I'll see you hear again," and under his breath, he sighs, "I hope."

The next night at ten o'clock, as Pablo sweeps the sidewalk, he sees John parking his white 2020 Toyota Camry a little closer than he had been parked the previous night. Again, Pablo keeps his eyes on him. On this night, however, John isn't watching him. Instead, he is busy looking at something in his lap, which Pablo assumes to be John's phone. Actually, John is doing this on purpose because he wants Pablo to believe that he is just sitting there. He doesn't want Pablo to know that he has returned in hopes of connecting with him again. After Pablo finishes sweeping, he returns the broom and dustpan to the diner, and eventually walks over to John's open window. "How are you tonight?" he asks John as he quickly glances down at the phone in John's lap. He sees that John is looking at Facebook. John looks up and into Pablo's wide eyes and says, "I'm good. How's your day been, Pablo?" "Good," says Pablo doubtfully with a half-hearted shrug. John, in somewhat of an effort to apologize for being here again, says, "I'm killing time on the way home from work. It's too nice out to go home yet." Pablo immediately notices a contradiction. Last night John said he was killing time on his way to work. Still suspicious of John, Pablo cuts the conversation short by saying, "Just wanted to say hello. Have to get back to the door." "Okay," says John, as he takes his wallet out and nonchalantly says, "I think I have a couple dollars for you, handsome." Pablo definitely notices the compliment of being called handsome by a man. He unsuccessfully tries not to react by twitching when John called him handsome. John doesn't see Pablo's reaction since his head is down to look in his wallet. Finding two singles, he discreetly casts his blue eyes down at Pablo's blue jeans' crotch and hands the money to him. John not only doesn't mind if Pablo catches him eyeballing his crotch, he kind of hopes he does. From past experiences, John knows that his unspoken clues can be much more effective than those that are spoken. "Thanks," says Pablo, as he turns to dash back across the street. John notices that Pablo doesn't use his name tonight, and he doesn't like that Pablo may have already forgotten his name. After all, John isn't going to forget anything he has learned about Pablo.

The next few nights, Pablo doesn't see John parked near the restaurant during the hours he is cleaning the sidewalk in front of the restaurant and panhandling. Though he is somewhat relieved that John, the man who very possibly has taken pictures of him, isn't around, he misses the nearly guaranteed handouts he may receive from him. Before a week passes, however, John returns. When Pablo sees John again, he doesn't know how long he has been parked along the street since his car is parked a further distance away due to the many cars on the block. Pablo considers whether he should walk that far away from the door where he is panhandling to talk to John. He obviously doesn't know how long John might talk, keeping him away from the door. However, he also knows John will most likely give him a couple of bucks. Suddenly, he sees John's car lights go on. He thinks John is going to drive away. He is certain that John is leaving when he sees John's left turn signal begin to flash. Needing a handout, Pablo extends his left hand in the air and yells, "Hey!" He jogs across the street and up to John's car as John begins pulling out of his parking spot. Pablo shouts, "Didn't see you till now." John shouts back, "Couldn't park any closer tonight. The restaurant must be busy with all these cars." "Yes, it's been a hectic night for carry-outs. Lots of people running in and out of there," says Pablo, and then laments, "People are in a rush, which makes it hard to stop them for handouts."

The truth is that John planned to circle around, pull up to the restaurant, double-park, and get Pablo's attention before giving him a couple of dollars. He definitely wants to keep in touch with this handsome man. Though he senses Pablo has already forgotten his name, he doesn't want him to forget him entirely. From his city travels, John knows that these homeless people tend to come and go. Some stay for years, of course, but most are here this month and gone the next. Additionally, John hopes to get to know Pablo as well as he got to know Luis, the last panhandler who held his attention at this diner. As John thinks about the risk of possibly not seeing Pablo again, he surprises himself by blurting out, "You have a telephone number for me, Pablo?" "No," says Pablo, and quickly adds, "Give me yours." John thinks this is great because, even if Pablo were to disappear from this location, there would still be a chance of hearing from him again.

A police cruiser slowly drives by and sounds the vehicle's loud and irritating horn to signal John to get back out of the street, as he is still pulled somewhat out of his parking spot. John puts his car in reverse and backs all the way back into his parking spot. Once the car is in park, he looks for something on which he can write his phone number. He finds a McDonald's receipt and writes his phone number on the back. After handing it to Pablo, he says, "If I don't answer, which I can't when working, leave a message and tell me where you are going to be hanging out. I'll get there as soon as I can. Or if you are going to be near the phone you use, leave a number and I'll call back as soon as I hear the message." "Okay," says Pablo. "Oh, and hold on," says John, as he takes out his wallet to hand him a couple of dollars again. After Pablo thanks him and dashes off, John drives on feeling a sense of progress now that Pablo has his phone number. Then he realizes that he missed his chance of discreetly reminding Pablo of his name, as he only wrote his phone number on the back of the receipt and not his name.

John debates how long he would wait before getting forward with his planned proposal for a date with

Pablo. He had success with Luis, but their relationship didn't last very long. It could have lasted a lot longer if John hadn't waited so long to let Luis know his intentions with him. It was just a couple months after they had finally begun dating that Luis disappeared from the streets. Luis likely had left the area by either getting into an anti-drug program or by being arrested. Possibly, Luis reunited with the girlfriend he used to talk about and moved back in with her. Whatever happened, Luis disappeared a good half-year ago and never returned to the street.

John is determined to get some dates with Pablo before he disappears for one reason or another, too. The strongest possibility that Pablo may vacate the nightly streets is that he might tire of the street life when the Chicago weather gets cold in a couple of months. Quite possibly, he will forgive his wife for cheating and move back home with her and his daughter. John knows he has to act skillfully, carefully, and soon. He has to act without pissing Pablo off, too. Though it's too soon to make an aggressive move on him, John knows he can't and won't wait too long, as he had done with Luis. John wants Pablo even more than he wanted Luis. Luis has a nice body and hot tattoos like Pablo, but Pablo is more handsome with his big, sexy, brown eyes and infectious smile. Though Luis has a deep, smooth voice that excites John, Pablo's deep, sexy voice sounds even more charismatic.

Chapter 3: Luis

Yet, John figures that Pablo is suspicious of him since he caught him taking his picture, which John has denied having done. That bump along the road to Pablo's zipper causes John to move in on him slower than he would like to move in on him. However, he can't move too slowly or he might miss his opportunity to have any dates with him. John's next step is to get Pablo in his car, go for a ride, and get to know him better. He tries to remember how he finally got Luis in his car the first time that they went for a ride to get to know one another. He can't remember. He does remember, however, where they eventually parked, talked, and had their first encounters. What he remembers most vividly is how Luis had no idea that John found him to be attractive and desirable until they took that first ride. In spite of being a long-time street person, Luis was extremely naïve concerning John. He was surprised to find that John is gay and that he had wanted to orally pleasure him.

During that first ride together, John was allowed to touch Luis' muscular legs freely. After the dejection from his girlfriend and family, he found that being desired by anyone in any manner was welcome to him. The second ride involved more touching, as Luis separated his legs far apart to give John's roving hand more access as they rode in the car. It wasn't until their fourth ride that John parked the car where neither of them could withhold the desired connection they had developed. Luis finally unsnapped the silver

Mexican-buckle on his thick, black leather belt and reclined his car seat slightly. Without words, John unsnapped the silver button on Luis' blue jeans and pulled down the zipper. He paused for Luis to continue the undressing, but he didn't. Yet, the solid print that bulged down the inside of Luis' left leg of his jeans shouted that he was ready to be enjoyed. John purred, "I want you so bad, Luis." At that, Luis raised his firm ass cheeks off the car seat, pulled his jeans down a bit, reached into his white briefs, and took his throbbing cock out for John. Without hesitation, John bent to his right, lowered his face down to Luis' crotch, and engulfed his hard, uncut cock deep into his mouth. Luis began moving his hips just as he must have done when fucking his ex-girlfriend's warm, wet, pussy in the past. At the sound of traffic coming down the dark side street, John stopped. "You almost got me," gasped Luis. After the vehicles passed, John went back down on him and let him continue fucking his face to his satisfied completion. They had an incredible, erotic escapade that John is now determined to revisit. This time, however, he wants the adventure to be with Pablo's cum filling his throat instead.

John can't get his mind off Pablo for the next couple of days. Therefore, he passes Cermak on his way home from work on this rainy evening in hopes of seeing Pablo again. Unfortunately, and not surprising due to the inclement weather, the objective of his lusty desire isn't there. Another panhandler who is facing the doorway and who is much taller than Pablo is there instead. John leaves the area. To his surprise, he sees Pablo and another man walking west near California Avenue. If Pablo were alone, John would stop to offer him a ride. However, the man he is walking with wears filthy clothes and has a huge red backpack on his back, which is even dirtier than his jeans. If Pablo were to accept a ride, the other man would likely want a ride, too, and John doesn't want the other man's filth inside his car. Furthermore, when he finally gets Pablo inside of his car, he wants to spend time alone with him. Consequently, he passes the two without being noticed. He has to wait for another opportunity to get to know Pablo better.

Several days later, John sees Pablo panhandling at the taco diner again. This time, Pablo is quicker to walk over to John's car to talk. He says that he has moved to a new place where he is staying with two other men under a train's deserted underpass, as the street where the underpass is located no longer goes through. "It's a dead-end street," Pablo explains. John considers the location for a moment and says, "Yeah, I know where that is. I've been down that dead end street a couple times when I've been cruising around at night to take a piss." By telling John where he is now staying during the overnight hours, he is suggesting that John can find him there. "Please don't tell anybody where I'm staying," adds Pablo. "Who would I tell?" John thinks. Regardless, John considers

Pablo's confidentiality as a huge step forward in attaining his trust.

Chapter 4: The Underpass

The next night, John takes a ride to the street that dead-ends at the deserted underpass. He stops his car a short distance from the haunted-looking structure before him and contemplates getting out and walking toward it. Just after he gets out of his car and quietly closes the door, he sees a small orange flame flicker in the far left side of the underpass' eerie darkness. Someone is there. John stands still and continues to watch. A long minute later, the orange flame is visible again in the same spot. Someone is lighting something. John gets back into his car and starts it up. He flashes his bright lights in hopes that Pablo is there, will see his car, and will walk out from the darkness. Nobody walks into view. He then sees headlights a block behind him in his rearview mirror. As it approaches, it becomes clear that it's a Chicago Police cruiser. Rather than come all the way down to where John is sitting in his car, the cruiser turns left, to the west. Deciding he doesn't have a good reason for being there, John gives up for tonight by making a U-turn and driving away from the underpass. When he gets to the main street, Roosevelt Road, he sees the police cruiser hasn't headed down Roosevelt. Instead, it turned into a large parking lot that John couldn't see from where he was parked due to shrubbery obstructing his view. The police are possibly waiting in the parking lot with their lights turned off to see if and when John would drive out of the conspicuous location where he had been parked. After engaging in a full stop at the stop sign at Roosevelt Road, John turns right, heads west, and decides to cruise around Cermak a while longer. He drives south on California, passing the vast darkness of Douglas Park until he arrives at Cermak Road. He cruises back east, passes the diner where Pablo panhandles, turns around near Rockwell Avenue, and heads back west. Unfortunately, John sees no sign of Pablo or anyone else who looks interesting. At that, he heads home for the night.

The next time John sees Pablo, just two days later, he tells him about his experience of checking out the underpass. Pablo confirms that he wasn't there at the time. He says that one or both of the other guys had to have been there, since John had seen an orange flame's flicker in the dark. "Probably both of them were there. They don't stray after dark," says Pablo. Though he is interested in the part of John's story about the police parking nearby until he left, he acts unconcerned by saying little about it, other than, "Yes, they sit there often." Typical of John, he wonders who the other two transients are and what they look like by asking, "What are the other two people who are under there like?" Pablo describes, "One is a quiet Mexican, and the other is a tough-acting Puerto Rican who I don't trust. And a white lady is there with the Puerto Rican a lot. She seems like a weird one." John wonders if he may have ever picked up either one of the men, or maybe even both of them, and asks, "What are their names?" Pablo says, "The Mexican never says a word to me. Not one word. The Puerto Rican and the girl probably told me, but I don't remember." Then he clarifies, "I'm tired when I get there. I find my spot away from them on the other side of the underpass, fall asleep, and leave when I wake up. I try to avoid them. I don't need to know them. As soon as I put some money together, I'll be out of there. I hear I can get a room around here for a couple hundred." Unfamiliar with room rates, John asks, "A couple hundred a week?" "No," says Pablo, "fifty bucks a week. I'm talking about a room to sleep in, which might have a roommate, a bathroom down the hall, and maybe some use of a kitchen. That's all."

Chapter 5: Tenochtitlan Plaza

John is curious about who the other transients are at the underpass. After all, Luis is far from being the only panhandler John has gotten to know well in the past. Pablo is just one of a good number of fine-looking men on the street that John has been interested in getting to know during the time he has cruised Chicago. John started working on the city's Southwest Side a few years ago when he got out of the community college in nearby Cicero where he got an associates' degree. He landed a decent paying job at a bank in Pilsen. He doesn't necessarily find his job interesting or even likable, but he gets along with his boss and the people who work with him well enough. Additionally, he makes more than enough money to pay his bills. Shortly after he got the job, he discovered the areas where street people, often Latinos who are about his age, hang out. Not all of them are transient or homeless, but many of them hang around outdoors rather than stay cooped up in their apartments. In particular, John finds Tenochtitlan Plaza to be interesting in good weather. It is located right near the bank, where 18th Street, Blue Island Avenue and Loomis Street intersect. After work, John strolls through the plaza and occasionally fantasizes about the men he might invite to go for a ride some evening. In time, he met Gerardo.

Gerardo, who John still sees near the plaza on rare occasion, was very perceptive when he first noticed John. He was quick to figure out that John was interested in him. Apparently, Gerardo had received John's type of hungry look by other men before, and he knew how to respond. The third time their eyes met, Gerardo smiled, broke from his gathering of locals, and approached John. After small talk, he asked for a ride. Naturally, wanting to get to know him, John agreed to give him a ride. After John started his car and asked Gerardo where he needed to go, Gerardo smiled an incredibly seductive smile and said, "Anywhere we can get away with it." John suddenly had second thoughts about doing something with someone who was often sitting at the plaza so close to his workplace. Yet, when Gerardo took John's wrist on his left arm and placed the hand on his black pants' bulging crotch, John didn't resist. At the conclusion of this first episode with Gerardo, he found that it wasn't all for pleasure on Gerardo's part. Driving back to the plaza, Gerardo unveiled his hard luck story of needing rent money. Though disappointed with the small amount John was able to provide, he didn't whine too much after only getting ten dollars. He assured John that he would need double that amount in the future. Though initially uncomfortable gifting someone with cash for sexual pleasures, some days after work, Gerardo's striking appearance with his dark Latino complexion, thick black hair, and attractive clothes was just what John needed before heading home. Though not often, John occasionally picked up Gerardo at the plaza. After they had parked along one of the block-long factories in the eastern portion of Pilsen, John gave him twenty dollars for a good time.

The experiences with Gerardo weren't only John's first pickup for a date in the area, but they were also his first dates in which he was hustled for cash for the dates. In time, with others, such occurrences happened once every few weeks. Continually being concerned about keeping the confidentiality of his escapades near the bank, as well as being uncomfortable with Gerardo's proximity to his workplace, John begins avoiding the plaza after work. Instead, he starts cruising to the west on 18th Street and Cermak Road when heading home from his job. In time, he discovers, the best place for cruising success is along Cermak. If he hangs around late enough into the evening, he finds the locals and transients gathered at underpasses off Western Avenue, behind buildings on 22nd Street, and in front of businesses up and down Western as well as along Cermak where they panhandle. When it is cold or rainy out, they gather at fast food places like McDonalds and Subway until a manager kicks them out for loitering. Though John infrequently dates anyone, window shopping for dates and giving the transients change has nearly become part of his daily routine. It is extremely rare that he has become infatuated with someone's good looks. However, when he wants someone bad, he is nearly obsessive with getting to know the man and in getting a date with him. Pablo is the first man in quite some time that he wants so much. Currently, his fantasies and desires for a date with him are as strong as ever.

Chapter 6: Nicky

A few nights after the last time he had seen Pablo, John parks along Cermak near the diner in hopes of seeing him again. Instead, another man walks up to his car, sticks his head into the passenger's side window, and startles him by yelling, "Hey, Johnny! Can I get in?" Instinctively, Johnny smells the beer on his breath and says, "Sorry, Nicky. Gotta run." Dropping his face and mustering up a desperate look, Nicky begs, "I need my medication, Johnny. Just ten bucks?" "Sorry, I can give you two," says Johnny as he takes out his wallet and sees only one single. Therefore, he takes four quarters in change from his change-holding cup holder. "This is all I can give you," says Johnny. "Thanks, man," says Nicky.

Nicky first hit the streets about a year ago when his wife threw him out for being a drug addict. He was gorgeous then. Now, after being on the streets for a year, the filth and smell of the streets have become embedded in him. Nicky liked John a lot from the start, and he was very accommodating and accepting of his gay lifestyle. Even though getting blowjobs from a man was a new experience for him, he was pleasantly surprised that he received great enjoyment from being aggressively serviced by someone who has such a hunger for him. When they met on the street, John was amazed at how Nicky didn't seem to realize how handsome he is. It had been obvious from the start that Nicky didn't understand how anyone, especially a man who appeared to be as decent as John is, not only wanted to perform oral sex on him but would pay him for engaging in the activity as well. John dated the light-skinned, six-foot tall, trim and muscular Puerto Rican at least a half-dozen times over the past year. He has enjoyed massaging his wide shoulders and muscular chest before going down on him. Nicky's chiseled face freely offers his bright smile along with a sparkling personality when he isn't too drunk or high. Though he isn't typically huge between the legs for a Puerto Rican man, he is definitely long enough and adequately thick. John loves his thick, natural forest of coarse black pubic hair, too. He rarely finds such an erotic sight with men's current trend favoring manscaping or shaving it all off. If Nicky would clean up, John would definitely date him again. However, it doesn't look like he's going to get his act together. His teeth are now yellowed from constant cigarette smoking, and he has developed a nasty smoker's cough that he didn't have when they met.

Naturally, John doesn't like that a former date is chilling where he has perched himself in recent times to find Pablo. If Nicky were to become a regular near the diner, the man's aggressiveness could challenge his cash donations for Pablo, and worse yet, could take his time away from Pablo. Pablo is the man in John's radar now, not Nicky or anyone else. With no sign of Pablo on this night, John takes off and decides to get some dinner on the way home. First, though, he decides to scope out the underpass where Pablo has said he is staying after dark.

Chapter 7: Jake

When John arrives at the underpass, he parks his car a short distance from the dead end again. He gets out of the car, opens both of his car doors on the driver's side, and takes a piss between them on the ground. He grabs tissues to wipe off his shoes after getting some piss on them and tosses the tissue aside as he closes the back door and climbs back into his car. He blasts WLS-FM, which is playing "Jump" by Van Halen in hopes of getting the attention of anyone who might be in the darkened underpass. In a shadow, he sees the silhouette of someone. The person is too tall to be Pablo. In an attempt to get the person to walk into view, John rapidly turns his bright headlights on and off twice. The figure appears again in the shadow but then quickly disappears to the right side of the underpass. While getting the nerve to turn his car off, lock it, and walk into the darkness to speak to the person, John hears faint voices from behind his car. He turns his car around and puts it in park. A woman and a man are walking toward him from Roosevelt Road. John recognizes the man, extends his left arm out of his window, and waves. The man, named Jake, waves back. When Jake and the woman get up to the car, John says, "Hello," to the two of them. The woman says, "Hi," and keeps walking toward the underpass as Jake stops and says, "Haven't seen you in a while. Can I get in?"

John knows that Jake is extremely aggressive in asking for a healthy handout. Also, Jake demands more than Gerardo used to settle for when giving up his humongous, throat-choking, Puerto Rican cock. Therefore, John lies to him by saying, "Sorry, I don't have time right now." Lowering his voice, John adds, "It's been ages since I've seen you on Cermak, Jake. Were you locked up?" "No," he says, "I got back with my wife but it didn't work out." He laughs and says, "She threw me out again." "Why?" asked John. "Fuck if I know. Can't figure her out," he snickered. Then he nods toward the underpass to where the woman had gone and half-heartedly says, "I'm with her now. She's all right." John drops his eyes to the six feet and four-inch-tall Puerto Rican's crotch, which is at his eyes' level as he sits in his car, and he sees a desirable sight. When he looks back up to Jake's face, he sees that Jake caught him taking a peek at the print of his thick cock in his pants. "Somebody said that a Puerto Rican was staying here, and I thought there was an outside chance it was you still on the street," John says. Jake offers, "Yeah, there's me, the woman, and a couple other guys, but I'm leaving here before long. I don't care for the other guys. They're difficult." John figures that Pablo is one of the other guys but doesn't want to let on that he knows him just yet. If John were to run into Jake again at this underpass, maybe he would ask about Pablo at another time. He fears Jake might link the two of them together, and, of course, Pablo doesn't know John is gay yet. John wants to eventually tell Pablo rather than have Jake boldly make a wrong assumption about Pablo and him dating.

John returns the next night, and Jake quickly comes out of the underpass. Desperate to find Pablo, who wasn't at the diner again, John says, "You know, the guy who told me that a Puerto Rican is staying here is named Pablo." Without skipping a beat, Jake says, "He's not here right now." Then he repeats the same question he asked the night before, "Can I get in?" "Sorry," just stopped by to check things out as I'm driving down Roosevelt again. Seeing a police cruiser pull in, John says, "I look suspicious back here. Gotta run." "Don't worry," insists Jake, and adds, "They come down this street all the time to take a break. They don't bother anybody." John asserts, "They're not always cool with drivers of cars. I've had more than my share of unwarranted stops and a couple bogus traffic tickets from them," and then adds, "I have to move on anyway." Before he drives off, Jake asks, "Got a few bucks to help me out?" John shakes his head in disgust and pulls all four of his singles out of his wallet, hands them to him, and takes off. A quick return trip to the restaurant to find Pablo is futile. On the way home, John has serious second thoughts about going back to the underpass to take Jake for a ride. He's still tall, muscular, and handsome enough, though he is in dire need of a good haircut. Then he talks himself out of dating him on this particular night because he really shouldn't be spending Jake's fee for pleasure right now.

More than a week passes before John cruises by the diner on Cermak and sees a couple of men standing down by the corner at Washtenaw. He backs into a parking spot and observes. Sure enough, the taller of the two men heads south on the side street and the shorter man heads to the doorway of the diner and stands with his back to John. The delightful sight of seeing the man widely separate his feet in order to spread his legs suggest that it is Pablo, as he often stands with his feet spread in such a manner. Within a short time, the man turns around, and John sees that the man is definitely Pablo. John powers his windows up, turns off the car, gets out, locks it, and quickly walks diagonally across the street to speak with him.

"Where have you been, Pablo?" shouts John as he nears the handsome man. "Here, but earlier in the day," answers Pablo. "Did you lose my number or what?" asks John. As Pablo tries to wrack his brain about having received his phone number, John continues, "You forgot I gave you my number?" "I did lose it," says Pablo. "Well, hold on to it when I give it to you again. I've been wanting to tell you about me going to the underpass. You're still there, right?" asks John. "Yes," Pablo affirms. John informs him, "I was there twice, and both times I saw Jake. I met him here on the streets a while ago. At first, I didn't mention your name, but the last time I was there, I asked about you," confesses John. "He didn't tell me," says Pablo. "Of course not. He wants the handouts for himself," reasons John. Then he adds, "And there's more to the story. Won't get pissed if I tell you?" "What do you mean?" asked Pablo. Just then, someone leaves the diner and Pablo turns to charm the women in hopes of getting a handout, but he fails this time. "I mean that I want to confess something to you, but I don't know you well enough to know if it might upset you," says John. Sounding paranoid, Pablo says, "What did I do?" "Nothing," John snorts with a laugh, "umm, it's more about what I want to do."

Realizing that he's irritating Pablo rather than winning him over, John finally lowers his voice to confess, "I want to take you for a good ride, and I want to take you for the good ride before you hear about me from someone else." Pablo looks utterly confused and asks, "Where we going when we go for a ride?" "We'll find a good place to park, if you're agreeable," says John with a lengthy silence to follow. Then he finally continues with the most-sultry voice he can muster, "I want to get to know you a lot better." "I don't know if I like the sound of this," Pablo hesitantly says. "Sorry to hear that," says John as he turns to walk away. Then he turns back to Pablo to chime, "If a guy doesn't ask, he'll never know what he can get, ya know." Before walking away dejected, he concludes, "Didn't mean to offend you. It was just an offer I hoped you'd accept." "Hold it," Pablo insists, and asks, "Have you taken any good rides with Jake?" John honestly replies, "I never talk about the people I've taken for good rides. I am discreet, just as I want my riders to be." "Sounds decent. I like that," says Pablo. John says, "I don't kiss and tell, don't suck and tell, don't swallow and tell." With the look of disgust, Pablo asks, "You swallow?" "There's one way to find out," returns John. Pablo extends his hand out to John and says as they shake, "Give me time to think about it." "Thank you," says John and boasts, "For the record, I'm good." As Pablo grins, John concludes, "I'll keep looking for you here rather than going to the underpass since I keep finding the wrong man there." Then he turns to the street, waits for a break in traffic, and jogs back to his car. Pablo doesn't receive a handout, as neither one of them thinks of it during the revealing conversation. In fact, John doesn't even remember to return to Pablo to replace his phone number. Instead, he quickly drives away while awkwardly still feeling the sense of accomplishment. After all, Pablo now knows that he wants him. Therefore, John can relax while the ball is in Pablo's court.

Chapter 8: Pablo and Jake

That night, Pablo returns to the underpass to find Jake and the quiet Mexican man already there. The Mexican is on his mattress and covered with a blanket from his neck down to his feet. His eyes are closed, though that doesn't mean he is asleep. Jake is pacing the length across the underpass, back and forth. From past experiences, Pablo knows Jake is stressed about something, as pacing is what he does when he's wound up about something. Pablo quietly sits on his mattress, opens a bottle of iced tea that he bought from the gas station down on Western and Roosevelt, and contemplates when he will talk to Jake about the man who has stopped by in recent nights. He wants to know more about him without prying too deep. He figures that all he has to do is mention that he knows the guy who has stopped by a couple of times in a white car, and then Jake will take it from there. Jake is a big talker and will probably talk endlessly, telling Pablo all he knows about him, without Pablo even asking one question.

About five minutes later, Jake stands still in front of Pablo and stares angrily at him. "Something wrong?" asks Pablo. "Fuck yeah, there's something wrong!" Jake bellows, and continues, "See that cop in the parking lot by the factory?" Before Pablo can answer, Jake says, "My woman's in his cruiser sucking dick!" "You're kidding!" says Pablo. "No. Sally told me she's been prostituting a couple cops, who pay pretty good, but now she's doing it right in front of me," says Jake. "I get paid for my dick sometimes, but I don't flaunt it in front of her," he cries. "Really? You prostitute yourself around here?" asks Pablo. "Why not? I got a big dick. I might as well use it to my advantage. Lots of people like a big dick," Jake snorts. Whether the right time or not to mention his acquaintance from Cermak who has stopped by a couple of times, Pablo says, "Tonight, I ran into a white guy I see a couple times a week on Cermak by the taco place, and he said he stopped by here and saw you. He knows you." "Speak of one of the devils," says Jake, and adds, "He doesn't pay much, but when I need my meds, I take what he's got and give him a good face-fucking." "So he pays for sex," says Pablo. "Don't play dumb with me. If you know him, you been taking blowjobs for cash," barks Jake. "No, for real, I never did anything with him, Jake. We just talk at the taco diner and he gives me a couple of bucks every time I see him. That's all," says Pablo.

"John is known in the area," says Jake. Suddenly, Pablo remembers the name he had forgotten. The white guy's name is John, he thinks. Jake continues, "I heard he was a cocksucker who paid for it before I finally approached him one night when he was sitting along 25th Street. He said he was parked there to take a piss, but I knew he was checking me out. Ten minutes later, I'm in his car with his head bobbing up and down in my lap for thirty-five dollars. After that first time, he only gave me twenty-five, I think. And fuckin' Sally is over there making at least forty bucks from each of the cops in that cruiser, fucking whore." After a period of silence, Jake says, "So that cock-sucking John quit me and is getting in your pants now." "No, Jake, I swear," says Pablo, and concludes, "We just talk, and I ask for a handout, and I get it." Jake lectures, "Then you're stupid. You could be making more than a couple bucks off him every time he sees you if you'd just get in his car and wait for him to proposition you." "I never did anything with a man before," confesses Pablo. "And you were never desperately homeless before either. Get serious, man!" says Jake. Honestly thinking out loud, Pablo says, "Don't know if I can do it with a guy, though. I'm straight." "I got news for you. He will suck it better than your wife has sucked you in years. He sucks me better than the bitch I married. He's damn good," Jake reveals with a grin. Pablo grins as he thinks of John boasting that he is good. Then he says, "Maybe, but I don't know." "Well, let him know he's wasting his time on you. Then he might let me in his car again," instructs Jake. "From what I hear, that cocksucker can't get enough. From what I see, the guy loves cock!" Jake announces.

Sally returns to the underpass looking satisfied and guilty. Jake asks her, "How much they give you?" "Not much," she says. As Jake raises his hand to slap her, he shouts, "Don't lie to me, bitch! How much?" "Stop it!" yells Pablo as he jumps up to potentially defend her. "Doesn't involve you, Pablo!" shouts Jake. Finally, Sally reveals money in her hands as she sobs, "One-hundred dollars, Jake. Each one gave me fifty." Jake grabs the money, takes a twenty-dollar bill, and throws the rest on the ground. Then he storms off to the north to buy his meds in Lawndale.

Chapter 9: Pablo and John

Three evenings later, Pablo is in front of the diner sweeping the sidewalk when he sees John parked a distance to the east. While sitting in his car, John writes down his phone number for Pablo again, as he realizes he never replenished his contact information after his last talk with Pablo. This time he writes his name beneath his phone number, too. He figures that even if Pablo doesn't approach him tonight, he will walk over and offer his phone number to him again, just in case Pablo wants to go for that good ride some night. After waiting no more than five minutes, John anxiously and uneasily gets out of his car, locks it, and saunters across the street. He slowly walks down the sidewalk until he is ten feet behind Pablo and says, "Hey, Pablo." Pablo turns to face him and, without his infectious smile, says, "Hey." John says, "The other night, I forgot to give you my phone number again, as I said I would." Pablo takes several steps toward him, reaches out his hand for the slip of paper with the phone number on it, and says, "Okay, thanks, John." Hearing Pablo say his name for the first time since the night they met tells John that he has been discussed, by name, with Jake. There doesn't seem to be any other reason for Pablo to refer to John by name for the first time in a month.

After an uncomfortable silence, Pablo asks, "You're done working for the day, huh?" "Yep," says John. "I'm just starting. Just got here," says Pablo. "What time you getting off work?" John whimsically inquires. "The usual, I guess. About midnight or so," says Pablo. "I could come back if you want a ride back to the underpass or wherever," says John.

Without giving the offer much thought, Pablo swallows his nerve and says, "That would be good, if you don't mind." While John is thinking he has found success, Pablo is thinking that he isn't sure he can do this. At least, he figures, he has a couple of hours, until midnight, to change his mind and disappear.

For the next couple of hours, Pablo is intently thinking about what Jake had told him. He said that John is good at sucking dick and that he paid thirty-five dollars the first time he was with him. Pablo convinces himself that he will try it. After all, he can give his right fist a much-needed rest by getting a good blowjob and he can definitely use the money. He decides that when John returns, he will tell him that he needs to go to the washroom in the diner before taking the ride. There, he will wash completely as he does most every night when the diner closes. Being clean, he will be much more relaxed and less self-conscious if tonight turns into the night he unzips his jeans for John. He wishes midnight and John would arrive soon before he changes his determined mind.

Twenty minutes before midnight, Pablo sees John parking a short distance from the diner. For the first time, John taps his car horn to let Pablo know that he has arrived. Pablo waves, holds the index finger of his right hand high in the air as if to tell John to wait a minute. Then Pablo scurries into the diner to wash up. He asks one of the cooks if he can use a cloth towel to wash up, as he wants to do a good job. With the soap dispenser appropriately stocked and the hot water running in the washroom, Pablo uses one end of the towel to wash his face, hands, and crotch well. Then he uses the other end to dry himself off. He then rinses the towel's wet end and soaks it with hot water to wipe off his entire head. Lastly, he dries his head off with the drier end of the towel. He looks into the dirty mirror scarred with gang signs etched into it and tells himself he is as ready as he can possibly be for the good ride. Little does he know that John is more nervous than he is.

After leaving the washroom, Pablo holds up the towel to the cook as if to ask where he should put it. The cook points to a dumpster at the far end of the counter. Pablo tosses it in the dumpster, thanks him, and says, "See you tomorrow night, I hope." "Good night out there, tonight?" asks the cook. "I've had better," says Pablo. "If you wait a few minutes, I can get something for you to eat," says the cook. "Thanks, but I have a ride waiting for me, so I better pass tonight," says Pablo. Surprised that the panhandler has a ride waiting, the cook says, "Oh!"

Once out of the diner, Pablo takes a deep breath and walks over to John's car window for permission to enter. He sees a hungry grin on John's face as John offers, "Get in, Pablo." John starts the car and asks, "You in a hurry to get back to the underpass?" Pablo jests, "Never." "Good. Then we have time to talk for a change," says John. "Can I get you something to eat from McDonald's or wherever?" offers John. "Coffee would be great," says Pablo, as he is too nervous to eat. "No problem," says John. This gives John more time to figure out how to delicately ask Pablo what Jake has told him about himself. After picking up two coffees in the drive-through, one for each of them, John parks in the McDonald's parking lot so both of them can add their creams and sugar packets. While parked, John says, "I'm curious. What did Jake tell you about me? He's a huge talker, and I figure he said something." "He's a big talker, all right," laughs Pablo. Then he adds, "I have a better question for you." "What's that?" asks John. Pablo asks, "What do you think he told me about you?" "Good answer," laughs John.

"Honestly," John continues, "I think he told you terrible things about me. He wants the two of us to not have a friendship because he probably thinks that I might end up wanting to hang around with you more than with him. He seems possessive in that way." "Oh?" responds Pablo. "So tell me," John asks, "what did you hear from him? You can trust me. I won't repeat it to anyone." Pablo considers this as John begins driving away from McDonald's. "He told you that I'm bisexual, didn't he?" says John. "Not exactly," says Pablo. "What exactly did he say then? I'd really like to know," says John. "Okay. He said you pay guys for sex and…" says Pablo, as John interrupts, "He has no right to say that. That's private between people." "So you really paid him for sex then?" asks Pablo. "I never talk to others about what I have done with people, and it's a promise I will keep to you," guarantees John. "I told you I want to take you for a good ride, and that good ride probably involves what Jake told you. Is that okay?" asks John. Looking to his side window, Pablo softly says, "Yes." "I don't want to do anything you're not comfortable with, Pablo. If you aren't comfortable, I won't enjoy myself," says John. Still looking out the window, Pablo mutters, "Okay." John reaches his open right palm with fingers spread, facing downward, and places it gently on Pablo's left pant leg halfway above the knee as he soothingly says, "Let's park somewhere."

At John's touch, Pablo's already tense leg tightens more for several seconds. Then he relaxes his leg muscles while allowing John to caress the denim softly with his fingers. "Relax," suggests John. To lighten the mood, he says, "I won't bite. In fact, I won't even scrape." He turns his caresses to more pronounced rubbing up and down a short distance of Pablo's upper left leg. "That okay?" asks John. "I guess," says Pablo. "Let's park down here," says John as he pulls to the side of a quiet side street alongside a darkened church. "Here?" asks Pablo. John says, "Sure. If we're not comfortable here, we can go elsewhere. I've parked here before to take a piss, to relax, or to just listen to the radio. It's usually very quiet here." Pablo's only response is to finally turn his head, look at John, and nod. "So, what's up, stud?" asks John. "Nothing yet," says Pablo. Moving his fingers from Pablo's upper left leg to his crotch, he squeezes his basket and says, "I can change that."

Instinctively, Pablo spreads his knees wide apart and allows John a good feel of his balls through his jeans. "I know everything works," says John, "since you told me you have a three-year-old." He adds, "Open your pants. I can get you hard." Though doubtful of the proposal, Pablo reaches to the left side of his seat and reclines a short distance. Then he puts the fingers of his right hand on his silver belt buckle, the fingers of his left hand on his black belt, and unfastens. After a slight hesitation, he unbuttons the silver button atop the zipper, which he then pulls down. John proceeds to search for the elastic waistband at the waist of his briefs and slides his fingers past a thick, welcoming patch of pubic hairs. He pauses to brush the forest with his fingers before traveling beyond his cock to cup his lightly haired balls. "Nice. Very nice," says John as he tenderly toys with each of Pablo's balls. Pablo slowly lifts his ass off the seat to pull his jeans and briefs down to his knees, which surprises John. He had not expected Pablo to so readily give such access to his naked crotch. A slight breeze in the night's air wafts an erotic, manly scent from Pablo's crotch, which enhances John's hunger for his cock. John softly asks, "Can you see in every direction?" Then he reasons, "I won't be able to see anything down there." At Pablo's non-response, John lowers the mirror on Pablo's side of the car and tells him to adjust it so that he can see the back view. Then he points to the side view mirror's control and tells him to adjust that mirror so he can get a good side view. Finally, John commands, "Keep your eyes open." John knows that some men like to close their eyes while being sucked, and during car sex is not the time to close them. John reaches his right hand up and squeezes Pablo's left shoulder, then brushes the bristles of his short hair on his head, and says, "Relax, handsome. I want you to enjoy this, too." "Yeah," says Pablo nervously.

At that, John bends over to his right as he slips his right arm behind Pablo's ass and deeply inhales the delicious scent of Pablo's crotch. Though Pablo had recently washed himself, his manly scent is present between his legs. John slurps Pablo's limp, uncut cock into his mouth and works its length with his tongue and sucking jaw, as he me moans with delightful at the feel of Pablo's plump, flaccid cock in his mouth, "Mmm." The vibration of John's voiced moan tingles Pablo's cock and it begins to react. John senses the positive reaction and moans deeper and longer while beginning to bob his head up and down slowly on his man's cock. The stiffening is accompanied by a more pleasing girth and length to Pablo's cock. John moves his left hand from Pablo's left leg and gently holds Pablo's balls as he continues to suck his shaft. At first, he gently massages his balls, knowing that some men don't care for ball play. Sensing that Pablo isn't overly sensitive there, John takes his mouth off the cock and takes his balls into his mouth. Pablo doesn't resist. Obvious that Pablo enjoys ball manipulation, John services his nuts for several minutes. After holding both in his mouth, he gently sucks one at a time before returning his hungry, warm, wet mouth to Pablo's stiffening cock.

With the head now poking out of the uncut skin of his fully erect piece, John places his wet lips on the crown and slowly licks at Pablo's cum slit. This sends chills through Pablo as he arcs his back slightly and pushes upward to let John know that he wants his cock inside of him. John gladly obliges by letting his wet lips slide down the entire length of Pablo's somewhat thick and smooth six inches of manhood. After his lips reach the black forest of hair above the shaft, John tightens his mouth and begins fucking Pablo with his mouth. He puts his right hand under his ass and pulls upward to let him know that moving his hips to fuck his face is not only allowed but also is desired. Pablo begins to fuck John's mouth slowly.

Before getting too involved, John briefly stops to ask, "You watching?" In deep breath, Pablo says, "Yes." Passionately, John returns to the base of his cock and sucks to his heart's delight as Pablo increases the speed of his thrusts into the back of John's throat. Minutes later, Pablo gasps, "Sure you wanna take it?" John moans, "Mmm," in hopes that Pablo takes that as an affirmative answer. He wants every spurt of Pablo's thick sperm in his mouth and eventually in his gut. Atypical of what John expects from this reluctant date, Pablo pushes down on the back of

John's head while lifting his body off the car seat. As the pulses of hot, thick cum start hitting the back of John's throat, John hears Pablo's "aaah, oooh, fuuuck!" John feels the explosions of cum traveling up and out of Pablo's tasty tool. After savoring the spent juices in his mouth with Pablo still in his mouth, John moans, "Mmm," while swallowing repeatedly. He slurps upward to the top of the shaft with his lips still wrapped firmly around Pablo's cock, not wanting to waste any of his cum. When John reaches the crown, Pablo flinches and yelps, "It's sensitive." John lifts his mouth off and says, "Sorry. I'll wash it off gently." He returns to the base of the shaft and does as he promised without disturbing Pablo's sensitive cock's head. Before sitting back up, he gently kisses along the shaft, which is beginning to return to flaccidity, and he finally plants a gentle, wet, parted-lips kiss on top of the crown. Pablo quickly pulls his pants up, begins redressing himself, and says, "Let's get out of here!" as if they are bank robbers taking off with the cash.

As John drives the short distance to the underpass where Pablo stays at night, he continually massages Pablo's left leg. John, of course, is still excited. He will remain excited until he goes private and jerks himself off while reliving tonight's sexcapade in his mind, likely in a dark place on his way home. At a red light, John reaches into his pocket where he has two twenty-dollar bills and two five-dollar bills. Knowing he wants to see Pablo again and again, he says, "I can't give you this every time, but I want to show you how grateful I am for this first good ride," and he gives him the fifty dollars. "Thanks!" says Pablo. When turning down the dead-end street that leads to the underpass, John says, "Maybe I should leave you out here," with the suggestion being that Jake might see them together at this late hour. Unfortunately, Jake is walking back from the gas station with a bottle of Orange Crush and a bag of hot chips. He sees Pablo open the car door. Before Pablo gets out of the car, Jake jogs up to them and shouts in an accusatory tone, "Where you two been?" John quickly answers just as assertively, "Gave him a ride from the taco place." "Nice try. The diner closes at midnight," says Jake. "Not every night," says Pablo. "Riiight!" says Jake with a sarcastic tone that clearly shows he doesn't believe them. He forges ahead toward the underpass without waiting for Pablo.

John discreetly says to Pablo, "He'll never know anything for sure unless one of us tells him." Pablo nods in agreement. John brushes the top of Pablo's head with his right hand's open palm as he instructs, "Hide the money. Don't let him see you spending it. And most of all, use my phone number soon." "I will. I promise," says Pablo. "Thanks, Pablo. I enjoy you a lot," says John. Pablo gets out of the car, taps his right jeans' pocket where he has stashed the cash, and says, "Thank you for this, John." Then he gleams a huge smile, vigorously grabs his satisfied crotch, and says, "And thank you for taking care of this!" As Pablo turns to walk to the underpass, John says, "Keep it warm for me, handsome."

The End

The Liquor Store Panhandler

By Wake Cruise

Chapter 1: Crim

Crim, a Two-Six gangster-wannabe, is a 36-year old, half-Puerto Rican and half-white drug addict who nuisances 26th Street in Chicago's Little Village neighborhood daily, unless he is locked up in Cook County Jail at 26th Street and California Avenue. The only times he isn't a fixture, either at one of the liquor stores' entrances or down at the McDonald's drive-through near the west end of the 26th Street business district where he shamelessly and aggressively begs for change, is when he is incarcerated at Cook County Jail. During the six years since his mother and stepfather finally threw him out of their home in Berwyn, a nearby western suburb of Chicago, he has been arrested at least a dozen times.

Due to his six feet and three inches of height, he is very noticeable among the Hispanics in the area. Typically, the Hispanic co-panhandlers are quite a bit shorter than he is. When he loiters the businesses and streets, he is head and shoulders above the others. He uses his height to intimidate most anyone. The times he has gotten into fisticuffs with men, however, he has ended up either backing down or getting the shit beat out of him. He is the product of a suburban family that never taught him how to fight in the big city because the family never knew how to survive the city. Yet, when they threw him out due to his history with cocaine, he ended up in Chicago where many other castaways continue to settle.

Even if it weren't for his height, one wouldn't be able to avoid his presence due to his loud and obnoxious voice, his overbearing laugh, and his disgusting smoker's cough. On the positive side, Crim is a very handsome man with his chiseled facial features, a thick and healthy head of black hair, and big eyes that can be quite engaging. Interestingly, his eyes' color is difficult to name, as they are somewhere between brown and green. His tall, trim stance and his overconfident, million-dollar walk are easy on the eyes. Being a good-looking man, however, is all that he currently has going for himself.

When Crim first got to Chicago, he used his real name, Jesse Gonzalez. After a couple of quick drug and loitering arrests by Chicago Police officers, he started going by an alias. Though he looks much whiter than Puerto Rican due to his light complexion, he has chosen to go by the name Carlos rather than Charles or any other white male's common name in English. However, the name Carlos has never stuck among the locals, including the 26th Street thugs. Due to his rapid succession of arrests, they call him Crim for criminal. The 10th District Chicago police officers even refer to him as Crim.

Miguel Gonzalez, who is no relation to Crim, instigated Crim's first arrest. Customers at Miguel's liquor store continually complain to Miguel about panhandlers hanging outside his business. In particular, many customers have targeted their complaints at Crim by saying something like, "The tall guy won't stop bothering me for change. He's intimidating. He blocks me from entering the store and then starts swearing at me when I don't have any change for him. Do something about it!" Miguel called the police a half-dozen times about Crim bothering his customers before they finally acted. One night, two cruisers showed up with four police officers at the store's entrance. When they confronted Crim, he denied he was doing anything wrong and that it is his right to stand on the sidewalk. One of the cops got in his face and told him to move along or he would arrest him. Crim walked a block to the west, turned to see the cops had left, and he returned to do his panhandling.

Within a few weeks, a half-dozen complaints later, the police finally followed up on their threat and took him in. Unfortunately, a couple hours later, after he was released from lockup, he walked back and defiantly parked his ass in front of Miguel's liquor store to panhandle again. When he returned, however, he eased his aggressive approach toward people. Surprising to Crim, he made the same amount of money panhandling when he wasn't so aggressive with people. Yet, he eventually returned to being a hard-ass again because he enjoyed panhandling much more when he was a tough guy.

Every evening when Crim collects a few dollars, he buys a cheap bottle of beer. Then he discreetly drinks it while hanging out on 26th Street. After he collects another ten dollars, he heads north to Lawndale to buy cocaine. Within a few hours, he returns, extremely high, and begins aggressively and desperately begging for more money. In his heightened state of mind, he conveniently forgets that being overly aggressive can get him in trouble, and he occasionally is reported to the police again for bothering customers or passers-by. Consequently, he has been given more rides to lockup.

Though Crim looked very young for his age when he arrived on 26th Street six years ago, he now looks every bit of his 36 years. On an extremely bad night, he looks older than that. Though the beer alone may not have taken its toll that quickly, the drugs and the street life have definitely affected him negatively. He's still very handsome when he isn't too fucked up, but his face has definitely started to show his age.

In time, Crim has found that he can make a quick twenty dollars or so along 26th Street if he drops his prejudice against gays and claims that he will do what they want him to do. A flamboyant man named Ernesto, who has often crossed paths with Crim on the street, introduced Crim to the life of quick and easy money. One night when Crim was extremely high and Ernesto was as horny as he usually is, the two began to talk down on the corner of Komensky and 26th Street. From previous encounters with Ernesto, Crim suspected that Ernesto wanted to get in his pants. "I think I know what's up witchoo, Ernesto," slurred Crim as he grabbed his basket between his legs. With a saliva-filled smile, Crim said, "Ya want dis, donchya?" With a smile, Ernesto said, "It's about time you caught on, Crim." "Follow me," said Crim. Ernesto walked behind Crim as he stumbled to the alley behind the liquor store and then went half-way down the alley to a couple of dumpsters that are sitting along the brick wall. Crim moved one of the dumpsters slightly so they could stand between them. Crim took his eight-and-a-half-inch cut cock out of his jeans, smiled with saliva drooling out the side of his mouth, and said, "Twenty bucks and it's yours, muh man. I'm giving you a deal, an introductory offer. Not because I like you, but because I need the cash bad." As Ernesto dropped to his knees, Crim grabbed his cock and put it back in his blue jeans, as he chuckled, "No, no, Ernesto. I wasn't born yesterday. I need the money first." Ernesto, frantic to get that cock in his mouth, took out his wallet, found three five-dollar bills and five singles. After Crim grabbed it, he carefully counted it and stuffed the bills in his right front pocket. He took his long, limp cock out again and said, "Make it quick. Ain't got all night." After no more than five minutes of tasting Crim's cock, Crim stepped back as he pulled his cock out of Ernesto's mouth, put his

semi-hard and wet tool back in his jeans and said,
"Gotta go, Ernesto." Ernesto protested that he wanted
more for his twenty dollars. Louder and more
aggressive with anger in his voice, Crim commanded,
"Said I gotta go, cah…!" He stopped himself short
from calling Ernesto a cocksucker. With that, Ernesto
headed down the alley to the east and turned to the
north when he got to Pulaski Road. His next stop was
in Lawndale. Though disappointed and pissed off, as
though he had just been robbed, Ernesto was still
horny as fuck. He stayed hidden between the
dumpsters until he successfully jerked himself off.
After having satisfied himself, he vowed he wouldn't
be paying for Crim's cock ever again, but he was only
lying to himself.

That is how Crim introduced himself to quick money
provided by the cock lovers who he has repeatedly
cheated along 26th Street. In time, he developed a
knack for spotting potential customers who weren't
flamboyant like Ernesto. In fact, he often senses when
some of the straightest-acting men, who he
encounters on the street, are cock hounds.
Furthermore, Crim is bold enough and desperate
enough for cash to make bold offers to men. Though
he doesn't grab his crotch and say, "Ya want dis,
donchya?" very often, he makes less suggestive
comments to offer himself for cash to potential
customers. On the rare occasions when he is offered a
good amount of cash, he more respectfully gives the

man more time than he gives Ernesto and his other twenty-dollar johns.

While cohabitating with other beggars in the panhandlers' turf along 26th Street, Crim bonds with some of them. Though he rejects the ones who live on the streets, he shares stories and gossips with the ones who are like him, in that they live in abandon buildings or rent very inexpensive rooms. Crim has been living in the same abandoned house up Pulaski, north of Ogden a short distance, for two years. The owner knows he's there but doesn't mind, as he considers Crim's presence as free security until he can sell the broken-down property.

The information the street thugs share with one another includes talk about the street cops, especially the undercover cops. They tell one another which cops are cool and which ones shouldn't be trusted or messed with. They also tell one another who, of the locals, is empathetic to their situation and who is quick to complain to authorities if they are bothered too much for their change. Additionally, they gossip about the suspicions they have of the locals they often encounter on the streets. They share their information or suspicions about the locals who buy or sell drugs, as many of the regular panhandlers are either alcoholics, drug addicts, or both. They share what they believe to be the preferred sexual activities and desires of some of the regulars on the street, as well as how much they will pay for sex. They know which prostitutes are real women, which ones are transvestites, and which ones are crossdressers. They know which men who hang on 26th Street late at night turn into male prostitutes when the price is right. They know what most prostitutes will do for their customers and how much they charge to do it. Most of all, they know which alleged prostitutes rob or cheat a potential john.

The male panhandlers who focus on a potential john don't try to proposition straight men, of course, especially the men who appear to be very committed to their marriage or relationship. However, they share their knowledge or strong suspicions of the men who are open to paying for sex. Like the other panhandlers, Crim gossips about the men who he suspects will pay for sex with a man, but he rarely admits that he has had sex with any man for cash or drugs. He is smart enough to know that he better not ever say a word about the couple of Cook County Sheriff's Department officers who have picked him up and paid him for his dick. Like practically all of the sex customers who panhandlers and prostitutes get, Crim is on the down low.

Chapter 2: Alejandro

The only panhandler who knows for sure that Crim has sex with a man for cash or drugs is Alejandro. Daniel, who owns a market in Little Village, had been sucking Alejandro's dick monthly for about two years when he asked Alejandro to get Crim to join in on the sex. Daniel told Alejandro, "That tall friend of yours in front of the liquor store looks interesting to me, if you know what I mean. Bet he's got a nice dick. How 'bout asking him to join us some night. I've had fantasies of one guy hitting my ass while another one feeds me." Alejandro tells him, "He's not really a friend of mine. I just see him sometimes when I'm out on 26th Street. But I'll see what I can do." Eventually, Alejandro confided in Crim about the offer, and Crim agreed to accommodate Daniel for a price. Since neither Alejandro nor Crim wanted Daniel's back door, they did a three-out-of-five coin toss. Alejandro lost. Therefore, the monthly activity involves Alejandro giving it to Daniel up the ass while Crim lets Daniel taste his cock. Consequently, Crim and Alejandro have become good friends and have openly shared their knowledge of who on the street is gay, the activities the johns want to do, and how much they will likely pay.

When their prostitution business is slow, as it usually is, they sometimes join forces in the middle of the night after the liquor stores and other panhandling locations have dried up. They walk through the neighborhood's streets and search for unlocked vehicles. They find many. They have stolen a few laptops, many nice pieces of clothing including leather jackets, and other items that can get a decent price on the street. They sometimes prowl down alleys in search of garages that are not secured well. Though they usually search for something of value to steal for reselling on the street, sometimes they just hang out and do drugs there. Like Crim, Alejandro has been locked up, but only a couple of times. All of Crim's charges have been related to his being a public nuisance while panhandling as well as for having been caught with small amounts of illegal drugs on him. Alejandro's arrests have been for stealing, once from a garage when the owner caught him and once for shoplifting at a shop on 26th Street. A couple of stores won't let Alejandro enter because they have caught him trying to steal or are just too suspicious of him while he's walking up and down the aisles of the store without ever having purchased anything. Actually, he has stolen from all of them several times before the stores finally refuse to let him in. Undeterred, he hops on a bus with his panhandling earnings and steals from stores in other neighborhoods, as there are plenty of stores in Chicago and the nearby suburbs for him to hit.

Alejandro is only 19 years old. He is a cute Mexican with a light olive complexion and big beautiful brown eyes. Though he much prefers women and gets them often, he is constantly horny and never has a problem with letting a man suck him off, if the man has cash or drugs to give him. Alejandro tells his johns that he's bisexual, but the truth is that he loves pussy and is, for lack of a better term, gay-for-pay. Crim is another story, though. He is definitely bisexual, though he admits that fact to no one, not to Alejandro or even to himself.

Crim isn't totally honest with Alejandro or anyone else. When he sees that someone is very interested in Alejandro instead of him, he tries to corner the john privately to tell him, "Be careful if you pick Alejandro up. He's only 17 years old." Most often, the john immediately drops his interest in Alejandro and pays Crim or somebody else for dick instead. Alejandro is no slouch when it comes to defending himself, though. If he were ever to find out how Crim is hurting his potential trade, bloodshed would likely follow. To date, however, Alejandro knows nothing about Crim's lies to potential johns about his age.

During the past spring and summer, Daniel has been calling Alejandro to stop by his place with Crim. Though both Alejandro and Crim have phones, Crim's is usually out of minutes or out of power. Anyway, when the call comes in, Alejandro has no trouble finding Crim on the street, usually near the liquor store after dark. While they are together, Alejandro calls Daniel back to set up a time, usually for nine-thirty the same day or the next day, as Daniel closes his market by nine o'clock and is ready for play at that time. The two cock salesmen show up to Daniel's market, as Daniel rents an apartment above the store space he rents. In his living room, Daniel strips down while Alejandro and Crim take their cocks out. As Daniel sits on his couch, the two stand before him as he alternates sucking the two cocks until they are hard. Alejandro is almost always hard before Daniel even begins sucking because he is always horny and ready for sex. Crim, however, is a different story. Often too buzzed on beer or drugs, as well as being disgusted by Daniel's effeminate posture, getting hard can be a challenge for him. Crim finds fellow-thugs attractive, not men like Daniel. He resists getting excited over Alejandro because he definitely wants Alejandro to believe he's totally straight. Alejandro, like other panhandlers, is a big gossip, and Crim knows word would get around if he acted like he was having male sex for any reasons other than the cash or drugs. On the street, more than anything, Crim wants to keep his self-proclaimed macho image.

Daniel takes a condom from a nearby end table's drawer and rolls it onto Alejandro's thick, cut, seven-inch cock. He then positions himself doggy style on the center of his couch. Crim feeds him his cock first. While Daniel is nursing Crim's tool, Alejandro straddles Daniel's ass and starts fucking. Alejandro and Daniel moan in ecstasy while Crim stays silent. Watching Alejandro close his eyes as he fucks, moans, and pants, Crim finally gets excited and becomes erect in Daniel's mouth. At this point, both prostitutes are jamming their cocks into either end of Daniel. When Alejandro is ready to shoot his mammoth, hot, thick load, he pulls out from deep within Daniel's ass and takes the condom off. Crim withdraws from Daniel's throat. All three of them know the routine. Daniel turns around to face Alejandro as Alejandro hurriedly puts his cock in

Daniel's mouth. Daniel loves his tart tasting cream and savors it all before he swallows deep. If Crim can cum and wants to cum, he sticks his cock in Daniel's mouth again. Usually, though, Crim just quits after Alejandro shoots his load in Daniel's mouth. The date ends with Daniel sitting on a towel on his couch while the two men stand before him again. He nurses their limping cocks, one at a time, in his jaw while he beats off with his left hand and caresses Alejandro's firm ass with his right. After he quickly reaches his own orgasm, he gives them each a minimum of twenty dollars and some treats from the market that he bagged for them. From there, Alejandro either goes to a liquor storefront on 26th Street to panhandle or to his family's residence while Crim always heads straight for Lawndale.

Chapter 3: Shark

On this late summer's night in early September, Alejandro is standing in front of a liquor store located further east on 26th Street. While he has the spot to himself, he spends more time looking at videos on his phone than he spends staying alert for handouts. A man, who is somewhat awestruck by Alejandro's good looks, passes him and enters the store. When he leaves with a lottery ticket, a two-liter bottle of Sprite, and a bag of Cheetos, he says, "Hey," to Alejandro. Typical of Alejandro's thinking he needs to lie to get what he wants, he chests his phone, casts a huge smile, and says, "Hello there!" Then, in an instance, his handsome face turns to a phony expression of grief as he says, "Some gangbangers robbed me, and I need some money for the bus." The man says, "Good they didn't get your phone, too." "Right!" says Alejandro, and adds, "That would have been worse! But they just took my wallet." "You tell the cops?" asks the man. "No. They won't do anything. They think I'm a gangbanger, too," says Alejandro. The man gives Alejandro a dollar, as he asks, "So what's your name?" "Alejandro. And hey, can you give me another dollar?" The man gives him a second dollar, as Alejandro asks, "And what's your name?" "Marty, but everybody calls me Shark," the man says. Before Alejandro asks, he explains, "I'm a damn good pool player, a pool shark. You know the expression pool shark?" "No, can't say I do," says Alejandro. "Since I'm a good pool player, a pool shark, the boys at the pool hall started calling me Shark. The name has stuck for a few years now." "Cool. Thanks for the two bucks, Shark," says Alejandro.

Shark walks down the street a half-block and gets in his car with his lottery ticket, soda, and a bag of Cheetos. As he tears the bag open and starts munching, he watches the handsome guy with whom he has just spoken. Alejandro successfully hits up another man for a handout and then walks across the street. Once across the street, he gets in the passenger's side of an old, multi-colored, partially rusted-out SUV that is sitting there. While facing west in his car, Shark sees the SUV that Alejandro entered pull onto the street and head east. As it goes by, he sees an old Mexican man driving. Naturally, Shark thinks it is odd that Alejandro lied about needing money to take a bus, and probably lied about being robbed, too. He asked himself why the panhandler wouldn't just ask for a handout without the bullshit.

A couple of weeks later, when Shark is stopped in traffic further west on 26th Street, he sees Alejandro standing in front of another store as he is once again looking down at his phone. Apparently, he is panhandling again, thinks Shark. He decides to reconnect with the cute guy. Though he has no reason to go into the store where Alejandro is standing, he can just walk in, browse, and come out. Better yet, he can just walk past him and stop to talk. Therefore, he parks his car, checks to see that he has a single or two in his wallet so that he can give Alejandro another respectable handout. He definitely wants to make a positive impression on Alejandro because he is approachable and possibly a future pickup for Shark. After all, Shark is no stranger to picking up men, and he would love to get in Alejandro's pants to see what he's got and what he can do with it. As Shark approaches the store, Alejandro looks up and immediately recognizes him. "Hey! Thanks for helping me out before, Shark!" says Alejandro. Not wanting to appear too anxious, Shark nonchalantly says, "Ah," as he grabs his brow as if he's thinking, and then adds, "Alejandro, right?" "Yes, you remembered," says Alejandro. "You didn't get robbed again, did you?" asks Shark. "Not since I met you. But I'm still broke," says Alejandro with a decent attempt at looking wretched. "I can help you out a little bit," says Shark. Again, he hands Alejandro a dollar, only to hear Alejandro ask if he has another one that he can have.

As Shark obliges, he asks, "You work?" "Not now. I have a criminal record, and it makes it hard to find work," Alejandro honestly reveals. "What did you do?" asks Shark. "What kind of work did I do or what did I do to get arrested?" asks Alejandro. Shark grins and says, "Both." Alejandro lies about the work by saying, "I used to work in a grocery store down Pulaski." Then he honestly adds, "About the criminal record, I didn't do much. A couple minor thefts. But it's still a record, which makes it difficult to get a decent job." Shark is impressed by his apparent openness about having been arrested, though he thinks Alejandro may have lied about the reason since he already has lied to him about needing bus money on the evening they met. "So what you do for money then?" asks Shark. "Whatever I can. Got anything for me to do?" asks Alejandro. Shark doesn't say what he's thinking but instinctively looks Alejandro up and down. "Give me your phone number and I can call you if I hear of anything," says Shark. Alejandro earnestly obliges by saying his number as Shark enters it into his phone. "Call me now so I have yours," says Alejandro. Shark does.

"How old are you?" asks Shark. "Twenty-one," lies Alejandro. "Maybe we can go for a beer some night," says Shark. Since Alejandro doesn't look to be all of twenty-one, he figures that he can prove his age by getting into a bar. Shark is thinking that Alejandro is twenty years old at the very most. Though he's a couple inches taller than Shark and has a good twenty pounds on him, there's something about his baby face that makes him uncertain of his age. Again, remembering that he lied about needing bus money on the night they met, Shark already knows Alejandro has trouble telling the truth at times. "And how old are you?" asks Alejandro. "Just turned twenty-seven," says Shark. "Happy birthday. My birthday is next week," lies Alejandro. "Well, happy birthday to you, too. You're a fellow-Virgo," says Shark. "Yep," he responds, though he has no idea what a Virgo is.

Chapter 4: At the Liquor Storefront

Cruising down 26th Street about a week later, Shark keeps his eyes open for anyone he might know or simply anyone he finds interesting to meet. After all, cruising around in the evening is his favorite pastime when the weather is nice and he doesn't want to stay in his apartment. His incentive to get out is that within a month or so, Chicago's colder weather will arrive. As he's driving past the liquor store, he sees a couple people standing in front. He searches for Alejandro, but doesn't see him there. Of course, he could call him since he has his number, but he said he would call if he hears of a job for him. He hasn't heard of one. Yet, he would definitely approach him again if he were to see him hanging out on the street.

Sure enough, when he passes another liquor store toward the west end of the 26th Street shopping district, he sees Alejandro talking to Crim. Shark has picked up Crim and given him blowjobs a couple of times in the past. He hasn't picked him up for quite some time though because he doesn't like that Crim is always in a hurry and ends dates abruptly. Shark likes to spend time relaxing with men, especially when he gives them decent money for their time. Therefore, he doesn't pick Crim up anymore. Though Shark doesn't gift every man he picks up, needy men in this area often ask for favors before going private.

Since Shark wants to see Alejandro but doesn't want to see Crim, he drives on without looking for a parking spot. As he drives by, Alejandro sees Shark and says to Crim, "The guy in the white car, you know him?" "Crim looks, recognizes Shark and his car but lies, "No." "He's gay," says Alejandro. He is shocked that Alejandro knows Shark, and more shocked that they must have had sex since Alejandro knows he's gay. Crim becomes determined to contact Shark and to tell him that Alejandro is only 17-years-old, even though he is really going on 20 years old.

The next several nights, Crim keeps an eye out for Shark to drive by, but it doesn't happen. Though uncomfortable in doing so, since he knows Shark isn't interested in him anymore, he searches for Shark's phone number to call him. He finds Shark's name and number are still in his phone's contacts, and he calls him. Getting voice mail, he says, "Shark. This is Crim. Remember me? Call me back." With no return within a day, Crim calls his phone again and leaves the message, "It's Crim again. I have something important to tell you. Call me!" These two calls are the first two times Crim has called him since they exchanged numbers as much as a year ago. Crim fears Alejandro might be related to the calls from Crim since he has seen Alejandro and Crim together in front of the liquor store. Beyond that, he has become increasingly curious to know why Crim is contacting him. Maybe he is just desperate for some money, Shark thinks. Though he doesn't want to date him again, he can help him out with a small handout, if that's all he wants. When he returns the call later that night, his call immediately goes to voicemail. Crim's phone is out of power. Therefore, Shark waits until the next evening to call him again and Crim answers.

"It's Shark. I'm returning your call. What's up, Crim?" Trying to sound businesslike, Crim says, "Oh, yeah, thanks for callin' back, man. Gotta see you." "I've got a lot of bills coming due like car insurance and shit, so I don't have a lot of money to burn right now," lies Shark. Though disappointed in hearing he might not get decent cash from him, Crim says, "That's all right. Somethin' I gotta talk to you about. It's important." "Tell me now," says Shark, and then adds, "on the phone." "No, I want, I mean need to see you," says Crim. Before Shark can say no, Crim asks, "You comin' down 26th Street tonight? I'll be there." Shark honestly says, "I could. But I don't like stopping when other people are there. I'm private. You know that." "Okay. When you see me near the liquor store, turn down the side street and I'll walk to you. Nobody will see us," says Crim. "I'll try," says Shark. "What time?" asks Crim. With frustration, Shark says, "I don't know. I said I will try to get there. I'm not even sure if I can make it." "Okay," says Crim as Shark disconnects the call.

The first thing Crim says to Shark when they meet face-to-face down the side street that night is, "People know you're gay, Shark!" "What? Who told you that?" asks Shark with surprise. "I was talking to somebody the other night when you drove by. The guy pointed you out and said you're gay!" says Crim. "Who? I can't even respond to this unless you tell me who is gossiping about me out here," says Shark. "His name's Alejandro," says Shark. In disgust, Shark yelps, "Alejandro? You've got to be shitting me! I hardly know the guy," says Shark, then defensively details, "I saw him panhandling twice and I gave him handouts both times. I am damn good to the guy. And he's talking shit about me? I can hardly believe it,

Crim! I never touched the guy." Shark puts his open palm to his forehead, slowly shakes his head in disgust, and then adds, "If somebody says that they think I'm gay because I cruise around a lot and look at men, that's one thing. But for someone to say I'm gay when he has no proof of it being true? That's just wrong, Crim!"

Loving that Shark is upset about this, Crim continues by pointing a scolding index finger at him as he says, "The other thing I wanna tell you is that you better be careful. He's only 17." Shark screeches, "Really? He told me he's 21." Crim responds, "He tells people that so they'll pick him up." Then Crim adds, "Since I helped you out with this info, how about helping me out with at least five bucks, man?" Shark knows that Crim is giving him this information in person rather than over the phone because he wants to be paid for allegedly helping him out.

Though disappointed in the news, Shark believes everything Crim has told him and obliges by giving him a five-dollar bill. "Make it twenty and we can do something right now. I found a great place to park down on 24th Street and Pulaski," says Crim. "You suggested that area before, and I told you that it's too risky and too dangerous in that neighborhood." "Nah, I was there last week with some black dude. He pulled into the alley on the west side of the Blue Kangaroo," counters Crim. "Blue Kangaroo? What's that? A nightclub?" asks Shark. "No, the laundromat on the corner," says Crim. "Okay, it looks like it dead ends back there," Shark says. Crim confirms, "It does." Then he explains, "The guy drove his car all the way to the end with his lights off. Nobody could see us." Shark says, "No way I'd drive in there! We could be trapped by gangbangers! And what do we tell cops if they ask us what the hell we're doing there?" asserts Shark. Then he adds, "And like I told you on the phone, I'm low on funds. So I can't be paying you for dick right now." "Well, keep me in mind," says Crim, and then he lies, "My balls are full and could use a good draining." When they part ways, Shark is very upset that Alejandro has been gossiping about him. He figures the thugs are rife with rumors on 26th Street, but he never would have thought that Alejandro, who has appeared to be so nice to him, is someone who is unjustly gossiping about him.

Chapter 5: Manuel Perez Jr. Memorial Plaza

The next couple of times Shark sees Alejandro on the street, he ignores him completely. He is so pissed off about Alejandro having told Shark he is gay, which implies that Shark has sucked his dick. Shark thinks that he can't trust these men with their penchant for gossiping and creating destructive stories. He also thinks that there is no way in hell he would have ever guessed Alejandro to be only 17. He wonders if the old man who gave Alejandro a ride on the night they met is one of his johns or maybe his partner in crime.

Doesn't matter, he resolves, as there is no way he is going to stop and talk to Alejandro again anyway.

A month later, Shark is parked alongside the Manuel Perez Memorial Plaza on 26th Street just east of Kostner. A couple of years ago, he picked up a hot Hispanic guy there. The man, named Miguel, has a wife and three kids. Typical of young married guys, Miguel was quick to figure that Shark had interest in him. One of Shark's ways of letting a man know he is interested is to call him the word guapo, which is Spanish for handsome. When Shark had first talked with Miguel at the plaza, he called him guapo a couple of times. Since Miguel hadn't been getting any sex at home for too long, he thought he would venture into new sexual territory. He also figured a white guy like Shark might even pay him for his cock. While it would be easy for his wife to assume if he was cheating with another woman, she would never ever think he was cheating with another man. After all, he has loved her pussy for years. Eventually, Miguel and Shark got together one night for a successful date in Shark's car. Several hot dates repeated until Miguel disappeared.

Several times, Shark walked through the plaza where he had initially found Miguel, but he was never there. In time, he tried calling him, but his phone was out of service. Months after Shark had last seen Miguel, he received a call from him. "In broken and excited English, Miguel said, "I in Tennessee. Big trouble." "Where in Tennessee?" asked Shark. "Nashville," returned Miguel in a panicked voice. Though Shark didn't fully understand the sketchy details of Miguel's problem, he agreed to take a road trip the next weekend to see Miguel. Due to his job, as he told Miguel, he wouldn't be able to drive down for a couple of days, until Friday, when he would get off work for the weekend. Actually, always having enjoyed road trips, Shark was looking forward to the long drive as well as having the opportunity to reunite with Miguel. By the end of the phone call, it was agreed that Miguel would call Shark back by Friday to say where they could meet in Nashville. However, that call never came. It's been at least two years since Miguel made that one phone call from Tennessee. Mysteriously, Shark has neither seen nor heard from Miguel since.

Anyway, while Shark parks alongside the plaza, recollecting his brief time in knowing Miguel, Alejandro appears at the open passenger's side window of Shark's car. Cautiously, Alejandro says, "Hello, Shark. May I get in?" Stunned by his presence, Shark yells, "Hell no, you can't get in! You're telling people I'm gay! I was good to you, motherfucker, and you're spreading shit about me!" Alejandro futilely screeches in denial, "What? What you talking about?" Shark has nothing more to say to him. Though he thinks of confronting Alejandro about the lie he told him about his age, he doesn't. He just starts his car and drives away.

If Alejandro were more honest, he would have told Shark that he is sorry he told Crim that he is gay. The truth is that he only senses Shark is gay because some of the men who are often most generous with the handouts on the street when they meet him are people who eventually pick him up. Another clue that makes him think Shark wants to pick him up is that he was so quick to ask him how old he is. He figured that question didn't just come out of nowhere, but was asked so that Shark would know if he is legal yet. Alejandro isn't that honest though, and he will never admit these things to Shark. He will just keep denying, with an unbelievable yet straight face, that he ever told anyone that Shark is gay.

Shark knows that he really doesn't mind if people know he's gay. However, hearing that such rumors are coming from a guy who has no such personal knowledge of his sex life really pisses him off. Shark shudders at the thought of Crim or anyone else thinking he is having sex with someone underage. Crim knows damn well that he would never do that. Sick of the gossip in the neighborhood, especially when the gossip is about his own personal life, he vows to quit cruising for sex along 26th Street until he gets over these frustrations.

Chapter 6: The Drive-Through

The next June, Shark is driving through Little Village and stops at the McDonald's near South Kostner

Avenue on the far western end of 26th Street's business district. Through the window, he sees the lines of customers waiting to be served inside are long. Therefore, he opts for the drive-through. After ordering his coffee with three sugar packets and a cheeseburger with mustard and extra pickles only, he sees a couple of men standing beyond the second window. They are standing where the panhandlers ask for the customers' handouts of change. When Shark pays at the first window, he tells the young lady at the cash register, "Please give me four quarters with my change so I can help the panhandlers up ahead." After he picks up his order at the second window, he sees that Alejandro, who is looking right at him through the windshield of his car, is one of the two men. Alejandro's eyebrows are raised while looking uncertain. Since Shark isn't as angry with Alejandro as he was when he saw him last fall, he doesn't ignore him. Instead, he just nods as he drives on. He drops his four quarters into one of his coffee cup holders for another time and other panhandlers. He figures it isn't beneficial to hold onto a grudge and to have enemies in a neighborhood where he has recently begun cruising again. After all, he is a white man, an outsider from the suburbs. Alejandro is the Mexican, a Little Village local, who possibly could make his life difficult through his connections on the street.

As Shark drives forward to McDonald's exit, he hears Alejandro finally speak. He shouts, "How you been, Shark?" Shark puts his left arm out of his car window with a thumbs-up to let Alejandro know that he is fine. Then he quickly drives on. Shark tries not to think about how damn good Alejandro now looks. He also tries not to think that since Crim said Alejandro was seventeen a year ago, Alejandro is now past his eighteenth birthday. In fact, since Alejandro said his birthday is in September, he is well past his eighteenth birthday. He has got to be legal. Yet, Shark tries to block these encouraging thoughts from his mind because he still doesn't trust Alejandro after he gossiped about him to Crim and possibly others in the neighborhood.

The next time Shark sees Alejandro along 26th Street in late July, they are both in the drive-through again. This time, it is late at night. Shark is vulnerable, as he has been unsuccessful when cruising for several weeks. Though he had a couple dates earlier in the summer, they were uneventful. In other words, he would really like to have a nice time with someone who really excites him. Seeing Alejandro on this night with a fresh haircut as well as a deep and darkened complexion from the summer's brutal sunshine, Shark feels a tingle in his crotch. Furthermore, Alejandro is dressed in a bright white t-shirt tucked into his nice-fitting blue jeans accompanied by a thick black leather belt, sparkling white Jordan tennis shoes, and a low-hanging silver chain around his neck. He looks so sucking sweet in his thuggish outfit that Shark becomes insanely excited.

As soon as Alejandro sees Shark, he cautiously walks up to the passenger's side of his vehicle while Shark waits for his order to be handed out the second drive-through window. Since Shark appears much more approachable than he had been the last two times he saw him, Alejandro leans over at the passenger's side window and softly asks, "Can I get in?" Shark looks in his big beautiful eyes, swallows hard, and says, "Okay. I have time to kill." says Shark. After he receives his order, he drives out onto the street, and parks his car. Shark offers to rip his burger in half to share, and Alejandro considers, "Thanks. I haven't eaten since this morning." Typical of Shark's goodness, he lies, "I really don't need to eat again." Then he says, "You have it. I'll just have my coffee." "Really? I can have it?" asks Alejandro. "Really," says Shark. As Alejandro digs into the burger, he says, "Man, they gave you a lot of pickles." "That's how I ordered it, with mustard and extra pickles only." "It's good like this. They musta made it fresh," says Alejandro as he thuggishly reclines his car seat and spreads his long legs at his knees. As he devours the cheeseburger, he asks, "How you been, Shark?" Shark responds, "It's kind of a boring summer, to be honest. All I do is work." "That's probably why I haven't seen you around," says Alejandro. Shark asks, "How about you? How've you been?" "Well, it's been kind of a tough year," says Alejandro. "I spent most of the spring locked up," he continues. "Where?" asks Shark with surprise. "Down on 26th and California, Cook County Jail," Alejandro replies.

"For?" asks Shark. "Same. Got caught stealing," he laments. Then he adds, "Without bail money, they kept me until the court case was settled. Almost three months in there. Now I'm on probation." "What does that involve?" asks Shark. "It's a hassle. Gotta check in with my probation officer once a month, and that goes on for two years. Actually, twenty-two more months. I gotta keep clean," says Alejandro. Shark thinks that means Alejandro is going to play things straight for a while and not even be interested in anything as adventurous as dating him.

Then their eyes lock. Though Alejandro is relatively young, he has been on the streets long enough to sense when someone desires him. Holding Shark's gaze, he thinks he is going to have success with him. If he were a betting man, he would bet that Shark is going to be his newest john. Breaking the silence and lengthy eye contact, Shark asks, "So you were in with the general population in County Jail?" "Of course," snaps Alejandro, "I'm gonna be twenty in a month-and-a-half. My juvy days are over." Juvy is colloquial for the juvenile detention center. "Ah," blurts Shark. Alejandro obviously forgot that he told Shark he was twenty-one years old a year ago. Now, in proper context, he is apparently admitting he is nine-teen. Therefore, thinks Shark, when Crim discouraged him from picking Alejandro up, he was already eighteen. It becomes obvious to Shark that Crim lied to keep him from dating Alejandro. Crim's conniving dishonesty doesn't surprise Shark at all.

"So you've been in juvy, too?" asks Shark. "Yeah, three times for the same shit. A man's gotta do what he's gotta do, ya know?" Alejandro unconvincingly claims. After he details endlessly about how he and his friend got caught taking things from stores on the Southwest Side, Shark asks, "You ever had a job?" Alejandro hesitates and says, "Well, kinda. I mean, I've done things for people who pay me money." After another hesitation, he admits, "But I never worked and got a paycheck every week." Wanting to end this conversation, he places his left hand on Shark's upper right leg and says, "So what's up?" Shark looks straight ahead rather than at Alejandro and says, "I'm a very private person, Alejandro. Being discreet and not getting tangled in neighborhood gossip is very important to me. I don't want men walking up to my car while thinking they can get a quick date or quick cash." Commandingly, he continues by turning to Alejandro and asserting, "I approach who I want to get to know, understand?" "Sure, I get it," says Alejandro. After a pause, Alejandro adds, "And you approached me." Shark reaches over and squeezes Alejandro's left shoulder as he admits, "Yes, I did." Alejandro sits up straight, puts his arms around Shark's shoulders, leans his face close to his right ear, and whispers, "Let's take a ride."

Not so ironically, Alejandro suggests the same location Crim had previously suggested along 24th Street. "Hmm," says Shark, and then asks, "You know Crim, right?" "Yeah, everybody does," says Alejandro. "He asked me to give him a ride to that area once, and I told him it's too dangerous with the possibility of gangbangers ambushing us." "It's all right," whines Alejandro. "No, not there," insists Shark, and then explains, "I hear about all kinds of shit happening in that area on the news and on the police scanners. I won't even stop there to take a quick piss anymore." Surprised, impressed, and convinced that Shark knows the area quite well for someone who doesn't live in the area, Alejandro concedes, "Oh, okay." As he returns to his thuggish posture, slouching down in his seat with his knees widely and welcomingly spread, he says, "Wherever you wanna go then." As Shark heads down 26th Street to the east, Alejandro takes Shark's right hand and puts it on his blue jeans where his throbbing cock is ready for action. "Anybody at your place?" inquires Shark. "My aunt is always home at night," Alejandro reveals. Then Alejandro asks him, "Your place?" "Nah, it's too far west of the city," Shark lies. The truth is that he doesn't want Shark or any other dates to know where he lives. It's bad enough some of his past dates constantly call when he is no longer interested. He definitely doesn't want them showing up at his door without notice. "Douglas Park is probably quiet," says Shark. "Sure," says Alejandro, "if you don't mind going that far." "Not far by car. At this hour, without traffic, five minutes tops," says Shark.

As Shark fondles him by lightly squeezing his hard shaft and rubbing his fingers up and down the lengthy piece, Alejandro unzips his pants and says, "I gotta let it breathe." He takes his cock out of his white Jockey briefs and his cock stands at attention. At the next stop light, Shark looks down and sees Alejandro's very thick, seven-inch cock. He holds it in his fisted right hand and says, "Nice." "Thanks," says Alejandro. Shark is surprised that Alejandro's cock is cut with a huge globe perched on top of the abundant shaft. Most of the Mexicans he has dated are uncut and not nearly as well endowed. Alejandro being relatively tall for a Mexican man, though, Shark thinks maybe that is why he is hung so well. His thumb gently glides over the slippery crown of Alejandro's cock, which is drenched with clear precum. He takes his thumb to his lips and inserts it into his mouth as he sensually groans, "Mmm."

Once to the park, there are several cars parked on the south end near 19th Street. Shark drives to the north end of this section of the park, just south of Ogden Avenue. The three cars there are vacated. He parks a distance away from the three cars and turns off his lights. Showing he has had experience getting car-sucked, Alejandro adjusts the rearview and his side view mirrors without prompting from Shark. Shark gets out of the car, takes a quick piss while scoping out the area, which is dimly lit by the distance white lights along the park's inner drive. When he gets back in the car, he says, "Looks good out there, but you've

got to watch for people walking out of the dark park."
"Got it," says Alejandro. "I figure you expect
something for this," Shark says, and then adds, "I
didn't plan ahead obviously." Alejandro interrupts,
"Whatever you can help me out with is appreciated."
"Good," says Shark. Then he informs, "The park
closed at eleven o'clock. Being the weekend, the cops
may be too busy to come by and kick us out. We just
have to watch so I can drive out of here if they enter
the park. I don't want a fine for being parked here."
From past experiences, Shark adds, "If we get
stopped, we say we just pulled in to take a piss. Then
we say, 'But now that you're here, officer, we will go
to a gas station to piss.'" Alejandro laughs. "You're
not going to turn the car off?" asks Alejandro. "No, in
case someone sneaks up on us, I can drive away faster
if it's running," says Shark. Then he adds, "And we
need to keep the doors locked and our windows
almost all the way up."

He looks at Alejandro and has the urge to kiss his
thick, supple lips. Putting his right arm around
Alejandro's shoulders, he takes his chin with his left
hand, draws him close, and kisses Alejandro like he
has never been kissed before. Passionately, their lips
part and the tips of their tongues softly meet. As they
both lean in for more intense mouth-to-mouth contact,
surprising to Shark, Alejandro is the first to moan in
ecstasy has he wraps his arms around Shark's torso.
When hunger for Alejandro's cock takes over, he
backs away from him and whispers, "I want to suck

the soul out of you, babe." "And I want to give it all to you," moans Alejandro in a tone deeper than his usual voice. At that, Alejandro leans back submissively as Shark leans to the right and deep throats the thick, long length of Alejandro's cock. With Alejandro deep inside of Shark, Alejandro groans, "Aaah, mmm, I need this so bad." As Alejandro breathes heavy on the back of Shark's neck, he tenderly places his opened left palm on Shark's back and gently runs it up and down his spine. Shark slowly moves his mouth and open throat up and down the length of Alejandro's pulsating cock as Alejandro's eyes roll back in delight. With all the quick and dirty tricks Alejandro has turned with men in Little Village, he has never been sucked so passionately by anyone. He realizes that this date is developing into so much more than just shooting his load to satisfy a man. This, he thinks, is what it's supposed to feel like. Equally, Shark is experiencing the giver's sensation as he has rarely felt with others. He feels incredibly connected to this man and his body.

He strokes the inside of Alejandro's thigh softly with his left hand as he tenderly and skillfully moves his warm, moist mouth with his velvety tongue. "Gonna make me cum in your mouth," purrs Alejandro. "That okay?" he continues. Shark moans, "Mmm," to signal Alejandro that he definitely wants all of his thick white liquid inside of him. Alejandro gently slides his hand from the middle of Shark's back to the back of his head to steady the gentle bobbing of his head. He then gasps and voices, "Oooh, oooh, yeah," as he begins to release himself inside of Shark. Shark swallows and then nurses his spent cock as it gradually softens, yet remains fully thick, inside of his mouth. He gently and firmly slides his mouth off Alejandro's meat and then kisses the shaft's length repeatedly. After one last deep-throated wash of Alejandro's beautiful cock with his mouth, Shark sits up and commands, "Relax while I do my own. I'm too hot to leave yet." Shark opens his jeans, takes his thick, six-and-a-half inch raging dick out, and begins to stroke. He turns to Alejandro and can't resist his mouth again. He reaches up to Alejandro's chin, and Alejandro submissively leans in for another long, tongue-laden kiss. Figuring that Shark could become a regular paying date, Alejandro definitely wants to please his newest partner completely. Consequently, Alejandro backs from the kiss and begins stroking Shark's dick for him. To Shark's delight, Alejandro whispers, "I'll get it wet for you." Shark sits up straight and watches as Alejandro takes him in his mouth. New to the activity, Alejandro gags slightly at the thickness in his mouth and throat opening. "It's okay. You don't have to," says Shark. Alejandro sits back up and they begin kissing again as Shark continues to jerk himself off to a glorious climax. They embrace tightly for a time before cleaning up and heading back to 26th Street.

At the end of the ride, Alejandro says, "I'll try to do better next time." "What do you mean?" asks Shark. Alejandro answers, "I guess I don't suck good." As Shark gifts him with two twenty-dollar bills, he sincerely says, "You are just what I needed tonight." When seeing the amount of cash he is given, Alejandro responds, "Wow!" Shark realizes that Alejandro doesn't get that much from other men who pick him up. Yet, for as much as Shark has enjoyed being with him tonight, he wants to please him. Shark tells him, "I've wanted this night since the first time I saw you. So I want to give what I can." Before getting out of the car south of 26th Street on Central Park Avenue, Alejandro initiates a long-lasting embrace and the night's last kiss. "Call me," Alejandro says with tender voice. Just as tenderly, Shark returns, "You know I will." After a pause, he firmly squeezes Alejandro's solid package between his legs and adds, "Keep it warm for me, babe." Alejandro guarantees, "You know I will."

The End

Wake Cruise's books include:

It Pays to Look Good

Men Wanted: No Experience Necessary

Seven and Seven

Cruising Little Village in Chicago

26276040R00076